D1018111

Elizabeth Gail and the Summer for Weddings

Hilda Stahl

Tyndale House Publishers, Inc., Wheaton, Illinois

Dedicated in loving memory of Kathy Souer

The Elizabeth Gail Series

Cover and interior illustrations by Mort Rosenfeld

Juvenile trade paper edition

Library of Congress Catalog Card Number 89-50675
ISBN 0-8423-0811-3
Copyright 1983 by Hilda Stahl
All rights reserved
Printed in the United States of America

3 4 5 6 7 8 9 10 95 94 93 92

Contents

ONE
A parting

The weight of his words bowed her thin shoulders and she sagged against the fence beside the horse barn, unaware of the blazing summer sun.

"If you do go, Elizabeth, that will be the end of us. I mean it!"

She could tell by the stubborn set of his jaw that he did mean it. She managed to push away from the fence as she forced back the hot tears stinging her eyes. "I am sorry, Jerry. I wish you could understand."

He pushed his large hands into his jeans pockets and hunched his broad shoulders. "I do understand."

"Then why are you doing this to me?" She folded her arms protectively against her rail-thin body. Snowball nickered from the pen, trying to get Elizabeth's attention. A car drove past on the road at the end of the long driveway to the Johnson farm.

"I must think of myself, too."

She studied the tall man who still seemed a boy to her. His dark eyes were full of pain and his dark hair was mussed from rubbing his hands over it. He was dressed in faded jeans and a short-sleeved knit shirt that showed of the muscles he'd developed over the years.

In her mind she could still see the thin boy dressed in ragged clothes, trying to hide the scar on his cheek. They'd lived in the same foster home, and they'd gone hungry and cold together. And been unloved.

Then the Johnsons had prayed her into their family and adopted her. She'd learned to love them and love God. Later Jerry had found a Christian family who loved him and wanted him. She and Jerry were close because of the past they had shared. They loved and understood each other.

"Elizabeth, Elizabeth. How many years have I put you first?" He rubbed his jaw and she could hear the rasping of his late afternoon whiskers. "You're nineteen and I'm almost twenty-one. We're not children anymore. It's time for us to have a life together, but you are afraid."

She reached toward him, then dropped her hand to her side. "I'm not afraid! I only want to establish my career before I get serious."

"Establish your career right here!" He waved his hand. "You have one of the best piano teachers in the world."

"I know Rachael Avery is fantastic, but she says that I need to be in school so that all my efforts are on piano. I have to go to Maddox School of Music. I do!" Why wouldn't he bend a little? "We both know my career can't suffer because of our love for each other." The pain in his dark eyes made her want to hug him and comfort him, but she couldn't allow herself that luxury. "I've given you extra time when you needed it."

A muscle jumped in his jaw and she knew he was trying hard to control his temper. "I had to graduate from high school, and that meant extra classes and extra study time, but that's past. I have a ten-hour-a-day job now and I want to spend my free time with you." He groaned. "But you want to move away! You want to go to school two hundred miles from here, and I won't be able to see you more than three times the entire time! Is that what you want?"

Numbly she shook her head, then whispered hoarsely, "I can't help it."

He swatted a fly away and she followed the movement of his hand and saw the white scar on the side of his face. Her stomach tightened as she remembered the day he'd finally told her about the scar. He'd never wanted anyone to know that his dad had slashed him with a broken whiskey bottle, and she'd never told his secret. He'd never told some of the terrible things that had happened to her while she moved from foster home to foster home.

Snowball nickered again, then ran across the pen, raising dust that tickled Elizabeth's nose. She glanced at her white mare, then looked back at Jerry. "Will you give me the time to study at Maddox?"

Goosy Poosy honked, then dusted himself in the loose dirt under the lilac bush.

Elizabeth glanced at the big white goose and remembered how years ago he had flown at her and knocked her down on her first day at the Johnson farm. She realized that her fear of the goose was nothing to the fear she felt over losing Jerry. She could see him struggling to reach a decision, a decision that was very important to both of them.

Finally he shook his head. "No, Elizabeth. I am ready for a lasting commitment. I want a girl who will spend time with me. I'm pleased that you're going to be a concert pianist. I know you'll be famous. But part of your time should be mine if you really love me."

She doubled her fists and her heart felt crushed beyond repair. "I will give you time when I get established in my career! I love you! You know I do!"

"You've been giving concerts around here. Can't you continue doing that?"

"Wayne Tyner will be my instructor at Maddox and Rachael Avery says that he is the best. And I'll have hours of practice time without interruptions." She wanted to throw her arms around him and beg him to understand, but she stood beside the fence with her head high, dying a little inside. Her shoulder-length brown hair felt hot against her slender neck. The peacock blue knit shirt with matching shorts clung damply to her.

"I can't live the next few years just seeing you occasionally," he said huskily. "Can't *you* understand?"

A tear slipped down her pale cheek and she quickly ducked her head. She could understand, but the fire that burned inside her was a greater force. She had to do everything in her power to further her career as a concert pianist. Nothing and no one could stop her. She knew absolutely that God's plan was for her to become a concert pianist. God had placed the dream inside her years ago, and she knew it was a dream that would come to pass.

"Is this good-bye, Elizabeth?" Jerry's voice was barely above a whisper and she thought he was going to cry, too.

She couldn't answer around the hard lump in her throat. She felt his hand on her arm, but she couldn't lift her head.

"Good-bye," he whispered hoarsely.

His hand tightened on her arm and the pain shot through her heart. She wanted to fling herself against him, but she couldn't move.

Finally he lifted her chin and her eyes met his. Tears glistened in his dark eyes and she felt the wetness of her own. "Good-bye, Elizabeth."

Her lips quivered and the tears slipped down and splashed on his hand. "Good-bye," she mouthed.

He lowered his head and his lips touched hers. She wanted to sway toward him and slip her arms around his neck and cling tightly, but she didn't move.

He cleared his throat. "I'll always remember you, Elizabeth Gail Johnson—Libby Dobbs."

She hadn't been plain Libby Dobbs for several years now and the name sounded strange, but very familiar on his lips.

Finally he turned and she leaned against the fence as he strode to his car. She wanted to call him back, but she couldn't speak. Snowball nuzzled her.

The white and blue Mustang drove down the long drive as it had many times in the past year since Jerry had bought it, then turned toward town. He would drive past Jill's house and she'd see and wonder how the serious talk had turned out. She and Jill had no secrets. They hadn't for all the years that they'd been best friends.

Jill would call or come down to hear the report and it would be too painful to tell.

Elizabeth sniffed and listlessly dabbed at her tears.

Jerry was out of her life. She loved him and he was gone.

The back door of the big white house slammed and Goosy Poosy honked, but didn't bother to get up. Susan stopped near the picnic table, then glanced toward Elizabeth. Did Susan know that Jerry had left never to return?

Elizabeth turned toward the barn, wanting to hide from her family. She loved them, but right now she needed to be alone.

She heard Susan run toward her. She stopped beside Elizabeth, her blue eyes filled with love and concern.

"I saw him leave," she said softly. Susan's long, red-gold hair swirled around her slender shoulders and her short legs looked very dark next to her white shorts.

Elizabeth barely nodded, then turned and gripped the fence rail, fighting against fresh tears. She knew Susan loved her as much as she would a real sister. Susan and Ben and Kevin were the real Johnson children. She and Toby had been adopted. She and Susan were both nineteen, but she was tall and thin while Susan was short and beautifully shaped.

She glanced at Susan, then quickly away. "He's not coming back."

"Oh! I am so sorry!"

Elizabeth nodded. "Me, too."

"Maybe you should forget about going to Maddox."

Elizabeth turned, her hazel eyes shooting sparks. "Never! How can you even suggest that?"

Susan squared her shoulders and stood tall, but even then only reached to Elizabeth's shoulder. "I never could understand your passion for piano! It's not normal."

"And what is? To fall in love with every boy who comes along? To go through life without a purpose and without a dream?"

Susan narrowed her eyes and clamped her hands on her waist. "I have a dream, Elizabeth Johnson! It just happens to be different from yours. I am going to be a wife and mother! I have had that dream as long as I can remember, and that is all I want! You're the one with the strange ambition of being a famous concert pianist. I am going to live an ordinary life with the man I love, once I find him, and I'll be happy!"

Elizabeth's hand trembled as she pushed her hot hair away from her thin face. Was she strange and different? Should she be content to stay home and marry Jerry and have a family? Could she do that?

Susan touched Elizabeth's arm. "I know you feel terrible about Jerry. I just don't know why you don't agree to what he wants. It doesn't seem unreasonable to me."

"He talked to you about this?" Elizabeth's chest felt tight.

Susan nodded. "He has to talk to someone, doesn't he? I told him he was right. You could stay here and study piano and be with him. What would it hurt?"

"It would hurt me!" She trembled. "I have to have the extra practice and instruction!" Her shoulders sagged and she felt bone weary. "Why should I bother to explain to you, Susan? You'll never understand. I thought Jerry would, but he couldn't either. And I am sorry."

Susan shook her head and her blue eyes flashed.

"No, you're not sorry at all! It makes you feel important to put your dream before anything else."

Elizabeth turned away, her hazel eyes wide with anguish. Was Susan right?

Susan stamped her small sandaled foot in the soft grass. "You go right ahead and be a martyr for your great cause! Jerry will find a girl who will love him more than she loves piano!"

Tears of sorrow fell inside her, but Elizabeth kept her face stony. She had learned to do that years ago when she was hurt beyond endurance, but didn't want anyone to know. "So, if that's what he wants, then let him. Maybe he should fall in love with you." The thought of that was almost more than she could tolerate.

Susan flipped her red-gold hair back. "Maybe he should! Maybe I'll spend my free time with him. I get out of work about the same time he does. I would sure know how to put him first!"

"Take him, then, the way you once took Joe Wilkens from me when we were little!"

Susan's face turned as white as her shorts. "I didn't take Joe from you, and you know it. It never got that far with you two because of your piano!"

Elizabeth ducked her head, her chest rising and falling. Why had she brought that up about Susan and Joe? Did she have to strike out at Susan just because her pain was so great? "I'm sorry, Susan," she whispered.

"Call Jerry after a while when you know he's home. Call him and tell him you changed your mind."

Elizabeth considered it, knowing the happiness it would bring, but she pushed the thought aside. "No,

Susan. I must go to Maddox School of Music. I have to learn all I can now."

"You're crazy!" shouted Susan, her head back and her eyes wide. "How can you toss Jerry aside that way?" With a groan Susan dashed to the house, slamming the back door behind her.

Elizabeth pressed her forehead against the hand that clung to the top rail. Snowball blew against her hair, but she couldn't lift her head or hug her white mare as she usually did. The sun burned down on her but she couldn't move even to step into the shade of the horse barn.

TWO
Surprise meeting

Applause burst around Elizabeth as she stood and bowed to the audience of Maddox students, friends, and relatives. She smiled, her heart almost exploding. This was her fourth—and best—concert in the school hall since she'd started Maddox over a year ago.

The applause continued. Mr. Tyner had said to play an encore if that happened. Elizabeth adjusted her long, silky-soft peach-colored dress, then sat on the bench again, her long fingers stroking the ivory keys of the grand piano.

A hush settled over the audience and Elizabeth played, feeling the music flow out of her. This was her life! Jerry was in her past, and with God's strength, she could live without him. She'd seen him once, then only at a distance, since they'd said good-bye. And that's the way she wanted to keep it because she still loved him, and seeing him was too painful.

Much later, Elizabeth walked with Chuck and Vera to a corner table in a small restaurant. "I'm sorry the others couldn't come," she said as she sat across from Vera and next to Chuck.

"They all wanted to come, but couldn't," said Vera, laying her purse in her lap. She was dressed in a burgundy suit and looked to Elizabeth the same as she had when she'd first seen her. Her blonde hair was cut short now and curled all over her head. Her blue eyes were full of pride as she smiled at Elizabeth. "I'm glad the concert was taped so that I can take a tape to the others."

"We're proud of you, Elizabeth," said Chuck, resting his hand on hers. His red hair had faded somewhat and strands of gray showed above his ears. "Have you heard from anyone who wants you to give a concert?"

She shook her head. "No, but I will!"

"I know." Chuck grinned. "You'll have so many engagements lined up that you won't be able to be home this summer at all."

"I'll make sure that I have at least a week with you." She saw a look pass between them and her stomach tightened. Before she could say anything the waitress came and took their orders. Hungrily she ordered shrimp and a salad. She could never eat before a concert, but she made up for it afterward.

Finally she leaned back and dabbed at her mouth with her napkin, knowing that her lip gloss was completely gone.

"Elizabeth, we have something to tell you." Chuck sounded very serious and Vera nervously crumpled her napkin.

"What, Dad?" Elizabeth locked her fingers together in her lap and waited. She knew it was something that would upset her just from the look on Chuck's face.

"I would've told you sooner, but I knew you were getting ready for this concert and needed all your concentration." Chuck cleared his throat and Vera moved restlessly.

"I can take it, Dad." Did they think she'd fall apart at the least little thing? Didn't they remember that this was the tough foster kid they were talking to?

"We both prayed about this and know that it's God's will," said Chuck, and Elizabeth sat very still as a shiver ran down her spine. "Two months ago I took Jerry Grosbeck as my partner in the retail business."

"Jerry?" Elizabeth whispered, her hazel eyes wide.

"He's been learning the business for a long time," said Vera. "And Dad really needed someone in the store. Jerry is perfect. Please, don't let it upset you. And please don't make it keep you away from home."

Elizabeth pleated her skirt with shaking hands. She tried to speak, but couldn't.

"Jerry also works with boys who need extra attention, boys in foster homes or in homes where there's no father." Chuck tugged at his collar and loosened his navy blue tie. "Jerry's a fine young man."

"Is he . . . is he married? Engaged?" Elizabeth tried to make her voice natural but she knew it squeaked.

Vera shook her head. "He doesn't go with anyone that we know about. He spends a lot of time on the farm." Vera reached over and patted Elizabeth's arm. "He talks about you, honey. He doesn't seem angry or upset with you. I don't think he'd be uncomfortable with you around."

"What about you, Elizabeth?" asked Chuck softly.

She took a deep breath. "I can handle it." She had no choice. She couldn't stay away from home because of Jerry Grosbeck.

"I know you can," said Chuck. "Kevin said to tell you that he'd write again soon, but he has tests all next week."

Elizabeth was glad for the change of subject. She laughed and it was almost normal sounding. "I always knew Kevin would become a detective. We'll call him 'Private Eye' from now on. And how about Paul Noteboom?"

Vera laughed gently. "You can't separate those two friends. But Paul has another two years before he takes his bar exam."

"I told him I'd hire him for my lawyer as soon as he passes the bar," said Chuck.

"I received a letter from Jill last month. She said she's working on a book. Do you see her much?"

Another look passed between Chuck and Vera.

"She hasn't been around lately," said Vera. "Maybe she's too busy with her book. Her dad says she's a very good writer. He said he'd recommend that his publisher accept her work for publication. She's counting on it happening."

They talked a while longer, then Chuck squeezed Vera's slender shoulder. "It's a long drive home yet tonight, so we'd better be going."

"I'm sorry you can't stay here," said Elizabeth as she picked up her purse and stood up.

"If I didn't have that appointment tomorrow afternoon, we would," said Chuck. "But it's a beautiful spring night and it'll be nice driving. I'll let Mom drive and I'll climb in the backseat and sleep."

"Sure you will," said Vera with a laugh.

Much later Elizabeth walked inside her dorm, her body aching and her head down. It was always hard to say good-bye to Chuck and Vera, knowing she wouldn't see them again for weeks.

"Libby."

She stopped, her head up, feeling like a startled doe that she'd seen often on the Johnson farm. Who called her Libby? That was a name from her past. Slowly she turned, then gasped. "Tammy? Tammy LaDere?"

Tammy nodded as she clutched a wide black purse to her thin body. She was almost as tall as Elizabeth, but had rounder curves. Her light brown hair fluffed around her shoulders and down her back. Her blue eyes looked scared. "I heard a long time ago that you were here, but I didn't have the nerve to come see you."

"I'm glad you came!" Tammy was her real cousin, and in the past they'd been mistaken for each other because they looked so much alike. But now Tammy looked tired and unkempt and much older than her twenty-two years.

"Is it too late to talk?"

Elizabeth was tired but she couldn't send Tammy away. "Come to my room. We can talk privately."

Tammy fell into step beside Elizabeth as they walked through the hall to the wide steps and up. "I heard your concert tonight. I didn't know you could play like that."

Elizabeth smiled at Tammy, then stopped at her door and unlocked it. "I've been studying piano a long time."

She clicked the switch and the small room was

bathed with a muted light. A single bed stood against one wall and a dresser and desk on either side of the closet. In one corner was a sink with a towel rack next to it with a bright orange towel hanging on it.

Elizabeth closed the door and offered Tammy a chair, then she sat on the bed, kicking off her high-heeled shoes. "Now, catch me up on you, Tammy. I haven't seen you since your mother forced you to go with her when I wanted to take you home for the Johnsons to adopt."

Tammy laughed nervously and pushed her hair back with a trembling hand. "I need help, Libby."

Elizabeth leaned forward, her hands locked over one knee. "I'll help you any way I can."

Tammy jumped up and walked to the window, then turned and walked back to her chair. She clung to the back of it and her face looked pinched and pale.

A nervous shiver ran over Elizabeth. "Tell me, Tammy."

Tammy tightened the belt around her black dress and brushed at the long sleeve. Finally she looked at Elizabeth right in the eye. "I'm going with a man and I just found out he's married. He's been lying to me since the day we met." Tammy slumped in the chair. "I really think he cares about me. And I love him! Oh, I know it's not right—going with a married man. I feel terrible! But I can't give him up. I can't! I wouldn't have anything left."

Elizabeth stood up and walked over to Tammy. She put her hands on Tammy's shoulders. "Tammy, if this guy really cared about you, would he have lied to you? You deserve to be treated better!"

Tears filled Tammy's eyes and slowly ran down the

side of her nose. "I can't help it, Libby I need to be loved. I'm so lonely!" Her voice ended in a wail and Elizabeth held her close.

Later Elizabeth once again sat on her bed and Tammy sat on the chair, her makeup gone from mopping up after the tears.

"Tammy, you have an emptiness in your life that no man can fill, not even if you were loved and loved him." Silently Elizabeth prayed for the right words as Tammy stared hopefully at her. "God made us, Tammy. He wants to fellowship with us. Until we fill that empty place inside with Jesus, we can't be happy.

"Tammy, you could go from man to man, you could be a wealthy woman, but you still wouldn't have what you're looking for tonight. You need Jesus as your Savior and Lord, and God as your heavenly Father. Jesus said that he came to give eternal life, abundant life. All you have to do is accept what has been given to you and confess Jesus as your Lord, and the empty void will be filled. You'll be given a new spirit inside and as you learn more and more about Jesus, you'll become like him. He is your answer, Tammy, not this man who is trying to convince you to do wrong."

Tammy dabbed at fresh tears. "I went to church for a while a couple of years ago and I heard about Jesus dying on the cross for my sins. I wanted to know more, but I quit going. I didn't know that this terrible need inside could only be met by Jesus."

"Shall we pray right now, Tammy?"

Tammy nodded and Elizabeth caught her hands in a firm grip.

Elizabeth prayed, then said, "Repeat this after me, Tammy. 'Jesus, I make you Lord and Savior in my life. I will leave my sin and follow you from this day forward. I believe in my heart that God raised you from the dead for me and I give myself to you. I confess you as Lord of my life. According to your Word, I am saved from death and brought into life. Thank you for making me new and for giving me your life, eternal life. I will live for you always and I will read your Word and become more and more like you. Thank you.'"

Several minutes later Tammy looked at Elizabeth, then burst out laughing. "You are looking at a new Tammy LaDere! I feel so clean and so wonderful! Oh, Libby! Thank you!" She hugged Elizabeth again.

"We've prayed for you all these years, Tammy." Elizabeth wiped away her tears. "I've thought about you often."

"Mother kept a close eye on me for a long time, but when I turned eighteen I walked out. I already had a job that paid pretty well, so I moved into my own apartment. It's across town from here. When I heard from Grandma LaDere that you were going to school here, I couldn't believe it. I'm glad I finally had the courage to talk to you."

"I am, too. We must take time to really get to know each other." Elizabeth laughed softly. "We still look alike, don't we?"

"Maybe I should take your place. I could be the famous concert pianist and you could work in Rooker's Manufacturing. Can you type and file?"

"Can you play the piano?"

"Chopsticks."

Elizabeth laughed. "I can type thirty words a minute."

"It's all set then. No one would ever know." She looked at her watch, then jumped up. "Oh, Libby! You must be worn right out. I didn't mean to stay this late. Do you have plans tomorrow? Could we get together?"

"Sure. How about in the afternoon?"

"I'll come get you about two and we'll do something exciting."

"Do you have a car, Tammy?"

"If you can call it that, but it does get me around."

"And Sunday we can go to church together."

"This weekend is going to be very different from what I thought." Tammy grinned as she picked up her purse.

"This is a new beginning for you, Cousin Tammy. I'm glad I could share it with you." Elizabeth walked quietly beside Tammy downstairs, but she felt like dancing and shouting. This was one night she'd fall asleep without thinking about Jerry Grosbeck.

THREE
Badden Lindsay

Elizabeth excitedly waved two tickets under Tammy's nose. "I finally got them, Tammy! You said two weeks ago that you'd go with me. I hope you still can."

"Tonight, you mean?" Tammy tugged at her hair, then looked down at her jeans.

"You'll have time to take a shower and change. Wear something of mine if you don't want to go home." Elizabeth opened her closet and pulled out a light blue dress. "This should fit."

Tammy held the dress to her, then looked at Elizabeth. "Why is this concert so important to you?"

"Tammy!" Elizabeth gasped in mock horror. "How can you ask me that? This man happens to be the best! Mr. Tyner has talked about Badden Lindsay since I first started here at Maddox. And now that he's in town, I must go. I didn't realize the tickets would sell out so fast, but I finally found someone who couldn't go, so I bought the tickets from him. I am even going to Mr. Lindsay's dressing room afterward to talk to him." Her stomach fluttered and she wondered if she'd really have the courage to do it.

"Is there any way he can help your career, Libby?"

"I don't know. I wish he could introduce me to the right people so that I would be invited to play at Grace Hall. That is an honor."

"Is that where we're going tonight?"

"Yes." She turned away, looking out the window at the rosy glow of the setting sun. Someday she'd play at Grace Hall. Someday she'd be invited to play in every state as well as foreign countries. Elizabeth Johnson would become as well known as Badden Lindsay. The thought almost took her breath away, but she willed it to be true.

"I think I will stay and get ready here, Libby. That way we can get to Grace Hall early just to soak up the atmosphere."

Elizabeth turned with a chuckle. "All right, Cousin Tammy. Tease me if you must."

Later Elizabeth walked beside Tammy from the parking lot to the door of Grace Hall. The May evening was warm and perfect. A few others had come early also.

A strange excitement filled Elizabeth as they walked down the carpeted aisle to their seats. The lone grand piano stood on the stage and she could imagine herself walking out on stage, bowing to the audience, then performing.

Tammy nudged Elizabeth. "The next time I come here, it will be to hear you play."

"And afterward we'll go out to eat with my family, and people will want my autograph and everything." Elizabeth's eyes twinkled and her wide mouth turned up in a grin. Gold loops dangled from her ears. Her brown hair was piled on her head and showed off her long, slender neck. Tonight she didn't care that she wasn't short and shapely like Susan. She felt gorgeous sitting in Grace Hall, waiting to hear Badden Lindsay.

When he finally walked out on stage in his black tails, she clutched her small purse so tightly her fingers ached. He looked younger than she thought he would. His dark blond hair touched his collar. He was tall and lean and had such a magnetism about him that her heart beat faster.

Applause broke out around her but she couldn't move her hands. Had she ever affected anyone this way? Lindsay's playing carried her beyond herself and at the intermission Tammy had to force her out of her seat. By the end of the performance she seemed to walk on air as they followed several others backstage.

"Maybe I should wait out front," whispered Tammy.

Elizabeth looked at her as if she'd forgotten she was around. "Don't you want to meet Badden Lindsay?"

Tammy shrugged. "Not especially. I know one famous concert pianist and that's enough for me."

"Then I'll see you out in front later. I won't be here long." She watched Tammy make her way through the crowd, then turned back. How could she hope to get a word with the famous man with so many others waiting? She wanted at least a little privacy. Tammy would understand if she didn't hurry right out.

Finally most of the crowd was gone and Elizabeth stepped forward, her palms damp, her legs weak. She wanted to rub her hand down her dress but she wasn't on the farm now. "I enjoyed your performance very much." She saw that his eyes were dark brown and as his hand closed around hers she suddenly forgot his name.

"Thank you."

He released her hand and she stood there, struggling to find something—anything—to say. Her mind seemed blank and she felt her face burn with embarrassment. Abruptly she turned and rushed away, almost colliding with someone at the end of the hall.

"What a shock! Libby Johnson?"

She turned and saw none other than her archenemy from high school, Joanne Tripper. She didn't look any different than she had on graduation day when she'd been angry that Elizabeth had been chosen to play the piano. "Hello, Joanne."

"Did you hear Badden Lindsay play?"

Badden Lindsay! That was his name! "Yes, did you?"

She nodded. "I talked to him earlier. He's taking me for coffee and a talk. I told him that I'd already played several concerts of my own."

Elizabeth bit her tongue and started away, but Joanne stopped her.

"Have you continued with your career, Libby? Or did you give it up when you realized you had no talent?" Joanne flipped her long blonde hair over her shapely shoulder. Her lilac-colored dress showed off her figure even more than she'd ever dared in high school.

"I have someone waiting for me, Joanne. Good-bye."

"Did I say something to upset you, Libby? Sorry." Joanne laughed and Elizabeth rushed away, her mouth dry and her blood boiling.

Tammy hurried to meet her. "Did you see him? Did

you talk to him? What great advice did he give you?"

Elizabeth fought against hot tears stinging her eyes. "Let's get out of here, Tammy," she said in a low, tense voice.

"What upset you? Will you talk to me?" Tammy practically ran to keep up with Elizabeth's long, angry strides.

Elizabeth jerked open the car door. "I can't talk, Tammy. Take me home and then come back tomorrow when I'm in a better mood."

Tammy drove through the traffic and Elizabeth sat in her seat with her shoulders slumped and her head down.

"Libby, whatever it is, you still have strength and help from your heavenly Father."

Elizabeth barely nodded. She had to get to her room where she could cry in private.

Tammy parked in front of the dorm, and caught Elizabeth's arm before she could escape. "Am I still going home with you tomorrow? To the farm, I mean."

"Is that tomorrow?"

Tammy nodded.

"I'll call you about it. I might wait and go later." Right now she couldn't make any decision. "Thanks for the ride, Tammy. Don't be upset about my actions. I'll be all right. I really will."

"After all you've done for me these past few weeks, I wish I could do something for you. But I will pray," she added softly.

"Thanks." Elizabeth turned and rushed to the door. A loving couple stood beside the door, wrapped in an embrace that made her think unwillingly of Jerry Grosbeck. Tonight she did not need that! She needed to think on something pleasant, something wonderful.

How could she be so stupid around Badden Lindsay? Could she really have forgotten his name?

She walked into the dorm and Belinda called to her and she had to stop. Belinda was her friend and she couldn't hurt her by ignoring her.

"How was the concert, Elizabeth?"

"The best I've ever been to."

Belinda tightened the belt of her robe. "I should've gone, but I had to practice my flute for our concert Sunday."

"I've got to get to my room before I collapse," said Elizabeth, inching away.

"Did you get your mail? There was a guy here to see you today and he left a message in your box."

A guy? Jerry? No, he wouldn't come after all this time. "Thanks, Belinda. I'll talk to you again soon. Have a good concert Sunday."

"I have a solo and I want it to be perfect."

"You'll do just beautifully, Belinda." Elizabeth gave her what she hoped looked like a smile, then hurried to her box. She pulled out a bundle of letters then realized that she'd forgotten for two days to get her mail.

Sounds of the TV followed her as she slowly walked up the wide stairs, flipping through the letters until she found an envelope with only her name on it. Her hand trembled and she sighed with relief. It wasn't Jerry's writing. But why should it be? Jerry couldn't still love her after all this time.

In her room she sank down on the chair at her desk, quickly opened the envelope, and briefly scanned the contents. Her breath caught in her throat and she dropped the letter on the desk. It was from the famous agent, Marv Secord, and he wanted to represent her! He said that he could book her in concerts all over, that he'd heard her twice already and talked to Mr. Tyner and even with Rachael Avery.

Elizabeth picked up the letter and read it again, this time slowly to make sure she hadn't read into it something that wasn't there. She carefully read the list of others that he represented. The name Badden Lindsay stood out as if it were printed in bolder type.

Marv Secord wanted to represent her!

She moistened her dry lips with the tip of her tongue and reread the letter. He wanted to meet with her tomorrow at three if she was free. Oh, she was free all right! Just wait until she told her family!

She pressed the letter to her and closed her eyes. This could mean that soon she'd be playing at Grace Hall. Her heart leaped.

"Heavenly Father, thank you for this letter. I want Marv Secord to be my agent, but I also want your perfect will. Help me to know deep inside if I should sign with him. Thank you for cheering me up. Forgive my anger toward Joanne."

Oh, just wait until Joanne learned about Marv Secord!

Elizabeth stood up and whirled around the small room, laughing aloud. Joanne would be livid. Livid! The tall, skinny aid kid was really making it.

Elizabeth glanced at her watch. She would call home. Chuck and Vera wouldn't care if she woke them up for this. Susan sometimes stayed up late and so did Ben.

She kicked off her shoes and grabbed the letter

again and rushed to the end of the hall to the phone.

Susan answered on the first ring.

"I have great news, Susan!" Elizabeth leaned against the wall of the phone booth.

"You met the man you're going to marry."

"Oh, Susan! Better than that."

"It must be pretty good if you couldn't wait to tell us when you get here tomorrow with Tammy."

Elizabeth gasped. "I forgot. I'm sorry I'll have to wait to come after school is out."

"But I was planning on talking to you this weekend about something very, very important."

"I'm sorry, Susan. But we'll sit down together later, I promise. Is Dad there? I thought I heard someone in the background."

Susan was quiet for several seconds. "Mom and Dad are in bed, but I'll get them if you want. Hang on. I'll be right back."

Elizabeth waited and she knew she looked strange, smiling from ear to ear in the phone booth. The minute Chuck answered she blurted out the great news.

"That's wonderful, Elizabeth. Your mom and I want the very best for you, and you must think this man is the best."

"He is, Dad."

"I'm glad for you, too," cut in Susan and Elizabeth wondered at the strain in Susan's voice.

"Tell the boys and Jill and everyone, will you? I'll call again tomorrow to let you know if I signed a contract with Marv Secord."

"We'll be praying," said Vera softly.

"Thanks, Mom. I love you all very much."

Elizabeth hung up and practically floated to her room. How could she sleep? Would Dad tell Jerry? Maybe Jerry would be so excited for her that he'd call, and they could patch up their differences.

She stood in the middle of her room and read the letter again.

FOUR
Happy news

Elizabeth dropped her toothbrush into the glass, then wiped her mouth. How could she sleep, knowing that in a few hours she'd meet with Marv Secord? But she had to so that she wouldn't yawn in his face.

She glanced at her desk where she'd carefully laid the letter, then shook her head. "How could I forget my other mail?"

She picked it up. "From Adam Feuder! I haven't heard from him in several months." She looked at the next envelope. "Joe Wilkens! What a surprise! And April and May!"

She carried the letters to her bed and sat cross-legged in the middle of the bed. "Now, I have a reason not to sleep. I'll read my mail instead of lying here staring at the ceiling." She spread them out on the bed, closed her eyes, and picked one. She wanted to read them all at once, but she picked up the one she'd chosen and turned it over. It was from April and it was quite thick. She ripped it open and pulled out the

folded pages. April and May Brakie were identical
twins and Elizabeth had known them for years.

Dear Elizabeth,

*I saw a ragged, scared little girl in the store today
who reminded me so much of you when May and I
first met you. The little girl wanted to buy a pair of
socks for her little brother but she didn't have enough
money. I wanted to sneak from behind the cash regis-
ter and get my purse and give her money but I didn't
dare. My boss caught me doing it last week and she
said she'd fire me if I did it again. If I didn't need my
job so badly, I'd quit.*

*How was your concert? I wanted to be there, but I
had to work. When you come here for a concert at
Kramer Auditorium, I'll be there for sure!*

*For the past three months I've been going with Adam
Feuder. I didn't say anything before because I thought
he would soon get tired of me, but I think he likes me
in a special way.*

*Elizabeth, I love him! I don't know what to do. If he
drops me and goes with someone else, I'll die! I wish I
could think of a way to let him know that I love him
without embarrassing us both.*

*Last night when he kissed me good night, I wanted
to stay in his arms forever. He is wonderful! He works
hard, so he doesn't have much time to take me out, but
we talk on the phone almost every night. I'd love to
live on the farm with him. I could learn to help him
with the chores.*

*He's been lonely since Grandma Feuder died. At
first he didn't want the farm that she left him, but
then he decided he wanted to get it going the way it*

had been when Grandpa Feuder was alive.

I haven't even told May how I feel about Adam. I think if I say it out loud something will happen that will keep Adam away.

I bought another plant for our apartment. May says it's like living in a greenhouse, but I like plants and this one is beautiful.

Your mom came to the store the other day to buy a blouse. She invited May and me to dinner Sunday and we plan on going. We'll follow them home after church. I wanted to suggest that she invite Adam to, but I didn't.

Jerry, of course, will be there. He doesn't seem like the same person that we knew when we were all foster kids. He is very mature, and works hard with your dad. The job really suits him. It was great of your dad to take him into the business. Since Ben wanted to run the farm instead of working in the store, Jerry was the perfect answer.

I saw Ben and Jill together at McDonald's a few nights ago. Are they going together again? I thought they'd broken up.

This morning I had my hair cut and styled for the summer. It's about shoulder-length and I feather the sides back. May still wears hers long so everyone can tell us apart now. I wonder if I had mine cut to keep Adam from making a mistake. I'd hate for him to kiss May and think it was me. He might like it better, and go with her.

It won't be long before you'll be home for the summer. We have a lot of catching up to do. See you soon.

Love,
April

Elizabeth grabbed the letter from Adam and quickly opened it. Did he have any idea that April loved him?

Dear Elizabeth,

Your concert is over and I'm sorry that I didn't get to hear it. Your folks said it was great. I borrowed the tape they brought back and listened to it. It sounded so different than the first stumbling songs you played on the Johnsons' piano. Even my mother, who was here on a flying visit last week, said you play very professionally. I think that she won't forget that you were an aid kid until you're interviewed on "Good Morning, America" or some other TV talk show.

Chuck and Vera invite me to dinner often. I think they feel sorry for me because I live here on the farm alone. I do get lonely.

That's why I'm writing, Elizabeth. You know April Brakie better than anyone else. Do you think she could ever love me enough to marry me and live here with me? She doesn't know what it's like to live in the country. I want to tell her that I love her and want to marry her, but I don't want to be rejected. Doesn't that sound immature? But that's how I'm feeling. I've prayed and I know God will let me know. Maybe he'll use you to give me an answer.

You and I have been friends since I was a frightened fourteen-year-old. I hate to admit it, but I'm frightened again. I want April as my wife. I couldn't handle it if she refused.

I've already planted corn and soy bean. Farming keeps me so busy I had to hire someone to take care of my other investments. I could hire someone to run the farm and live in the city. But that wouldn't suit me at all. Maybe I'd do it for April, though.

Talk to me when you come home, please. I wrote so that you'd have time to think about this and pray. You're a good friend.

Adam

Elizabeth folded the letter and chuckled softly. Adam and April had no problem, if only they knew it. She tapped his letter thoughtfully. She wouldn't wait until she got home. She'd call him and tell him to be brave and talk to April. Adam and April. They really did make a good couple. It would be great to have them living down the road from the Johnson farm in Grandma Feuder's home.

With a sigh Elizabeth remembered the hours she'd spent with Grandma, making cookies or just talking. She hadn't really been grandma to anyone but Adam, but everyone had called her Grandma. She would've approved of Adam and April.

A car honked and Elizabeth knew she wasn't the only one up so late. She looked at Joe's letter, then May's, and decided to read May's first. The paper crackled as she pulled it out of the yellow envelope.

Dear Elizabeth,

School will be out soon for you and for me. I love all these little first-graders, but I will be glad for summer vacation. I've signed my contract so I'll be here next year also. But I will have a new last name. I hope.

Joe Wilkens and I are in love and want to get married this summer. But—and isn't there always a but? But April and I have always said we'd have a double wedding. April says she doesn't know if she'll ever marry. Some days she's so down. I think if I tell her that Joe and I are going to be married, she'd really be down.

Elizabeth, I love Joe very much! When I first met him years ago, I never thought we'd some day get married. He sold another house yesterday and the closing will be soon. He's using his commission to buy a house for us. It's small, but we love it. It's close enough to school that I can walk.

I want you and April to be my bridesmaids. Will you? Joe is going to ask Ben to be his best man. Also Jerry Grosbeck. Can you handle that? We won't do anything until we hear from you. Joe will ask Adam if you don't want Jerry.

April and I heard the tape of your last concert. It brought tears to my eyes. We've come a long way! A few years ago April and I were runaways and you hid us in the horse barn. Now, we're all grown up! Praise God for his goodness to us all!

I'll talk to you when you get home. I'll look forward to seeing your cousin Tammy. See you soon.

Love,
May

Elizabeth pressed the letter to her and tears glistened in her eyes. Joe and May. Susan had gone with Joe a long time, and it seemed natural to link their names. How would Susan feel about Joe and May?

It was strange that Susan hadn't married yet. She had said that she wanted to marry and have a family. Did she go with anyone now?

Joe wanted Jerry in his wedding.

Elizabeth bit her bottom lip. Could she walk down the aisle with Jerry standing there? Would Jerry agree to be in the wedding if he knew she would be, too? Would he ever forgive her? Did he think about her as often as she thought about him?

She opened Joe's letter and forced thoughts of Jerry away. It seemed strange to think the boy down the road from their farm was selling real estate and soon to be married.

Dear Elizabeth,

I thought about you today when I got a letter from Brenda. Remember the time you socked her in the nose and made it bleed? Would the famous concert pianist do that?

Brenda is going to have a baby in the fall. She is very happy as a minister's wife, and with the baby on the way she is even happier. She might be home a while this summer.

She said she'd come for the wedding.

May Brakie and I are in love and want to get married. I'd like to get married now, but she wants to wait until school is out. This summer we will get married, even if I have to elope with her.

I teach the junior boys in Sunday school now. It sure keeps me studying my Bible, which is a good thing. I found myself going days without reading, but not any longer.

Jerry brings four boys to church with him every Sunday. They are foster kids who have never been loved. Jerry knows how to love them and I am learning.

I know May wrote to ask if you'd be in our wedding. Please say yes. We'll try to plan the day around your

*concert tour. Your parents told me how great you
played, so I know it won't be long until you have a concert tour that will keep you busy for years.*

*I sold Rachael Avery and her husband a big house
on the east side of town. With their three children, the
other house was too small. She made sure there was a
special room for her baby grand piano. When she
learned that you and I are friends, she said that she
didn't think she'd ever have another student as bril-
liant as you. Of course, I agreed. See you, Libby.*

*Your friend,
Joe*

Slowly Elizabeth folded the letter and slipped it into
the envelope. Time was passing very quickly. Just
yesterday she and Joe had ridden horses together
across the hills and pastures of the Johnson farm.
They had played softball and Ping-Pong and Mo-
nopoly. Soon Joe would be married.

Tears blurred her vision as she laid the letters on
her desk. Would she ever marry?

Her pink nylon nightgown tangled around her hips
and she stood up and let it fall into place. She
reached for the light, then stopped and picked up the
letter from Marv Secord. She read it once again, and
her world shifted back into place. Marriage wasn't for
her now. She had a career to establish and Marv Secord was going to help her with it.

The next afternoon at three o'clock she walked into
his small office. His blonde secretary had said to go
right in. She stopped just inside the door and looked

at the man standing beside the window. This couldn't be the famous Marv Secord. This man wasn't much taller than Susan and he was dressed in faded jeans and a red pullover shirt. The lower part of his face was covered with a dark, well-trimmed beard and mustache.

He stepped toward Elizabeth, his hand out. "You are Elizabeth Johnson. I'm Marv Secord." He had a pleasant voice and a firm handshake. "Come in and sit down."

"I was surprised, but pleased to get your letter," she said as she sat in a comfortable leather chair while he leaned against his desk.

"I hope you don't have an agent yet, Elizabeth. I know I could do a lot for you, and you'd be a great asset to me. I know of six theaters that would pay you handsomely for performing for them. Soon I could have a world tour for you. I don't have to tell you that you're good. You know it and your teachers know it."

She listened to him, hardly grasping what he was saying.

"Before you sign with me I want you to know that I'm a Christian. Jesus Christ is first in my life, my wife and baby are second, and my clients are third. I'll work hard for you, Elizabeth, if you take me on my terms."

She smiled, suddenly relaxing. "I'm a Christian, too, Mr. Secord."

"Call me Marv."

"Marv. I'm a Christian and Jesus is first in my life—even over my piano. I wouldn't want it any other way."

"Do you have any marriage plans?" Marv walked around his desk and sat down. His gray eyes were serious as he waited for her answer.

She shook her head. "I won't marry until my career is established."

"And will you continue with your career?"

"Yes. I could never give up piano. Not like Rachael Avery did." Elizabeth leaned forward earnestly. "My dream is to be a famous concert pianist. And I mean to be one!"

Marv smiled as he stroked his beard. "I have a contract here for you to sign. You can take it home and read it and bring it back Monday."

"Thank you." She wanted to grab it and sign it immediately, but she knew she had to read it first.

"Is there anything that you want to accomplish that I should know about, anything concrete?"

Elizabeth hesitated. Should she tell him? Finally she lifted her chin and looked right at him. "I want to play at Grace Hall."

Marv laughed with a nod. "I like that! Grace Hall. Badden Lindsay just played there and he is a big name right now."

"I know. I want to play there."

"Then you shall!" Marv walked around and held his hand out to her. "It might not be this year or next, but you'll play at Grace Hall."

She stood up, towering over him and shook his hand. She already knew she'd sign the contract, that this man would be her agent. "I'll see you Monday, Marv."

"Fine, Elizabeth. I must rush now. I told my wife I'd take her shopping this afternoon. Tell my secretary to give you an appointment as early on Monday as you can get here."

Elizabeth walked out with her purse over her shoulder and the contract in her hand. She'd just made one more step toward her dream.

FIVE
A new beginning

On Monday morning, Elizabeth walked eagerly into Marv Secord's office, the signed contract folded in her purse. "Good morning, Naomi." On Saturday, the secretary had asked Elizabeth to call her by her first name.

"Good morning, Elizabeth." Naomi smiled as she held a pencil midair. "Have a chair, please. Mr. Secord will be with you shortly. He has someone in with him now."

Elizabeth sank down on the brown leather chair closest to the door and crossed her long legs. She rubbed her skirt over her knees, then leaned back with her purse on her lap, her hands folded over it. Did she look too anxious? Could Naomi tell that she wanted to do cartwheels around the room?

The phone rang and Naomi answered it and it reminded Elizabeth of the call she'd made to Adam. He'd been very surprised to hear from her.

"I just wrote you a letter," he'd said.

"I know. I read it last night. I'm really glad that you

49

love April. I think you should go see her tonight and tell her how you feel. I think you should plan a summer wedding. I'd say sooner, but I want to be there." He'd caught his breath in a sharp gasp and she'd laughed aloud. "Did I shock the socks right off your feet, my friend?"

"I have to sit down before I fall down. Why do you think I have a chance with April?"

"Take my word. I don't want to say anything more, but just take my word. And tell May your plans."

They'd talked a while longer and Adam had agreed to tell her the outcome of his conversation with April. She looked across the room feeling very pleased with herself about Adam, Joe, and the twins as well as her career.

Just then Marv's door opened. A tall, thin blond man walked out with Marv right behind him. The man was Badden Lindsay! Elizabeth wanted to sink through the floor, but she sat very still with a smile pasted on her flushed face.

"Good. Elizabeth, I'm glad you're here. I want you and Badden to get acquainted."

She stood up and she wondered if her legs would support her. Would he remember her? That was too awful to consider.

"Elizabeth Johnson. Badden Lindsay." Marv sounded as proud as a new father. He looked very short next to Badden.

Elizabeth held out her hand and Badden's large hand closed around it. He smiled, and she managed to smile back.

"I'm looking forward to hearing you play sometime," said Badden in a deep, but soft voice. "Marv was telling me about you."

"I heard you play the other night," she blurted out. "I could've listened all night." Oh, why had she said anything about being at the concert? Now maybe he'd remember how awkward she had been when she met him backstage.

"Thank you." He turned to Marv and Elizabeth was able to breathe again. "I'll see you next month, Marv. Keep in touch."

"I will. Enjoy Perth and Brisbane and Melbourne." Marv turned to Elizabeth. "Badden has wanted to play in Australia for a long time, and his dream is finally coming true."

"That's wonderful. I know they'll love you."

He turned his dark eyes on her again and she felt weak all over. "Thank you. Good-bye." He nodded slightly, then said good-bye to Marv and strode out the door.

Elizabeth suddenly realized why he had looked so different. He wasn't dressed in a ruffled shirt and tails, but in jeans and a Western-cut blue plaid shirt.

"Well, now, Elizabeth, shall we get down to our business?"

She turned to Marv and blushed as she realized how it had looked for her to stare after Badden Lindsay. "I signed the contract, Marv." Did she sound breathless?

"I'm glad to hear that." He ushered her into his office and closed the door. "You won't be sorry."

She pulled out the contract and handed it to him. "How soon before I'll have a booking?"

He chuckled as he opened a folder. "I'm glad to see you this eager. Your enthusiasm and your willingness to work hard will help you to succeed in this competitive business. Many others have talent, but they don't want to set aside everything else in order to get to the top. Rachael Avery convinced me of your dedication." He tapped a paper inside the folder. "I only have to make a phone call to book you at Kramer Auditorium. People in that area are familiar with you. You'll pull in an audience and in the meantime we'll get to work letting everyone know just who Elizabeth Johnson is."

She listened to every word and tried to burn it into her memory so that she could repeat it to Tammy, then later to Chuck and Vera.

Later in her room she told Tammy, "And then after he said all that, he said that he'd call me in a few days and tell me where else I'll be going. He said that by the end of summer I'd have a full schedule!"

"Oh, Libby, Libby." Tears sparkled in Tammy's eyes. "This is one more step for you. I'm so glad! I think I want you to make it just as much as you want to."

"Thank you. I can't wait to get home to tell my family."

Tammy locked her fingers together. "Libby, I know I said I'd be able to stay two weeks with you on the farm, but I can't." Elizabeth started to object, but Tammy stopped her with a raised hand. "I can't help it. Mother is going to be here, and I must spend time with her. At first I wasn't going to, but then I knew that the Lord wanted me to show her love. She needs Jesus as much as we do. And he loves her!"

Elizabeth nodded with tears in her eyes. "I'm sorry that you can't stay on the farm with me, but I do understand. If you can come later, then do."

"I will." Tammy twisted her hair around her finger.

"I just wish I knew why Mother is coming now. She said that she and Jack were going to stay in California. Maybe she dropped Jack. Or he dropped her."

"I haven't heard about my real mother for a long time. Does Phyllis know where she is?"

"Marie Dobbs doesn't get along with us, Libby. I don't know why. I did hear that she was in Arizona for a while." Tammy sighed as she leaned back on the chair near Elizabeth's desk. "I wonder what we would have been like if our mothers had been like Vera Johnson? I guess it doesn't do any good to wonder. We are who we are." Tammy grinned and pointed at Elizabeth. "And just look at you! You are becoming a famous concert pianist! Several years ago you had no future, no hope."

"I'm thankful that the Johnsons prayed me into their family. They said when they went to see the social worker who is now my Aunt Gwen, she told them of kids who needed homes. When they heard my name, they knew I was for them. They prayed me to them. But it was a while before I could trust what I thought was my good luck. For a long time I thought they would send me packing. But they never did. They gave me their love and their name."

"I once was very jealous of you. It seemed like you had everything and I had nothing but misery. Now, I have Jesus and I have everything!"

Elizabeth nodded in agreement.

"Is Friday your last day of school, Libby?"

She laughed. "It sure is! I've loved being here, but it will be great to be finished. I'll still practice several hours a day, but I won't be graded for it. I'll have to find a place to practice. I don't think the family can stand four or five hours of piano a day."

"Do you think you'll get an apartment in town?"

"I'll talk to Dad and Mom and see what's best." Having an apartment of her own was a whole new thought. Right now she wouldn't think about it. It made her feel homeless. She needed a home base.

Music drifted in from someone's radio and Elizabeth looked around her small room, suddenly realizing her time at Maddox was over. Other students would practice long hours on the piano she'd played on. Would Marv Secord want to represent any of them?

Tammy walked to the door, then turned. "I'll be here Friday afternoon to pack your things into my car, then stay for the graduation ceremony."

"I'll send some of the things home with Mom and Dad. Are you sure you don't want to ride with them instead of us driving?"

"No. I'll drive, then I can come back when I must. The time alone will give me a chance to get it all together before I see Mother." Tammy wrinkled her nose, said good-bye, and walked out.

Elizabeth stacked her music books neatly on the end of her desk. Soon she'd pack everything and go home to the farm. It would be as if she'd never been a part of the room or the school. This way of life was behind her. A new life was opening up. She was no longer a student. She was a pianist. A concert pianist!

She walked to the mirror above the sink and stared at the reflection of the slender young woman with curly brown hair that touched her shoulders. The light green of her blouse brought out the green highlights in her hazel eyes. The wide mouth was still pink with lip gloss. "Hi, famous concert pianist." She wrinkled her nose and laughed. "Soon you'll be playing in front of thousands of people. Soon you'll be as well known as Badden Lindsay and you'll play at Grace Hall. And he'll come backstage and shake hands with you and say he enjoyed your performance." Elizabeth leaned closer to the mirror. "And you'll remember his name and he'll remember yours!"

SIX
A letter from Jill

Dear Elizabeth,

*I'll bet you didn't expect to hear from me this close to
your homecoming. But I wanted to tell you my news
and you know that I can express myself much better—
plus remember details—when I write instead of talk.*

*Sometimes when I'm down, I look in the mirror and
still see an overweight adolescent, instead of a slender
girl who is trying to become a woman. But I only feel
down when Ben doesn't call or my writing doesn't go
smoothly.*

*The book I'm writing is basically a love story and
I'm working on the second draft of it. Don't you wish
you'd been here to help me with this one the way you
did when we were in high school? Remember how I
used to keep what I'd written locked away in a special
box? I'm still very careful with my work, but I don't
lock it away and hide it in my closet. Dad says my
work is very well done, and he wants me to continue
writing. It is a wonderful career, and I enjoy putting
words together to bring people and plots to life. If I*

could manipulate my private life the way I do the life of the girl in my book, I'd have it made!

I hear Dad calling me, so I'll see what he wants and be back later to finish this letter.

Dad wanted to show me the contract for his one-hundredth book! That was worth being interrupted for. He and Mom are going out for dinner to celebrate. I wonder if I'll sell a hundred books by the time I'm forty-six.

Later in the summer Dad and Mom are going to Maine. Dad bought a cottage for them, and they're looking forward to spending summers there.

Paul won't be home for the summer since he has a full-time job. It is funny to think that my little brother will be a lawyer.

Now, back to Ben.

Where shall I start? Elizabeth, my very dearest friend, I want to share my feelings with you, but sometimes it's hard. Sometimes it's hard to know my feelings and admit them to myself.

Remember when Ben dated Christy Long? I wanted to yank her black hair out at the roots and smash in her gorgeous face, but I knew that wasn't exactly Christlike. So, I managed to keep my hands to myself. For a while I thought Ben was going to ask Christy to marry him—then she started dating Dave Boomer. You probably heard that they were married last month. That noise you heard was me shouting.

That day I walked down to the Johnson farm (knowing that Ben would be at the house at that hour). He was sitting at the picnic table with a glass of orange soda, and he looked as if he'd lost his last friend. His red hair was the only bright thing about him.

"Hi, Ben. Is this a picnic of your own, or can I join you?"

"Sit down, Jill." He sounded impatient and I almost turned and left, but instead I sat down and folded my arms on the table and looked at him.

"You've been working very hard in the fields, Ben. Give yourself a break and go to McDonald's with me tonight."

He laughed. "And is McDonald's a treat?"

"Sure. I know you like their french fries."

"How do you know that?" He offered me a drink of his soda and I took a sip and handed it back. I wanted to walk around the table and sit beside him and lean my head on his shoulder. Oh, but he's handsome! And strong and kind and wonderful!

"I remember how you used to beg my fries after you'd finished yours. I'll be glad to share my fries with you tonight."

He was quiet a while, then nodded. "I'd like that. I'll pick you up at seven."

"I'll be ready."

I tried on five outfits when I got home. I decided I couldn't wear my long green dress to McDonald's, so I finally decided on my navy dress pants and a yellow, pink, and navy blouse that really does look good on me.

When Ben drove in I forced myself to walk, not run, to the car. Did you know he just bought a new Chevette? It's a brownish-gold color and I love it! Anyway, I sat on my side very prim and proper. What else could I do with bucket seats?

"I asked Susan to come with us, but she had a date." I nodded to let him know I heard while I was silently thanking Susan for having a date. "Who's her date?"

"I don't know. Sometimes I think she's madly in love with someone."

Aren't we all? "Do you know who?"

"My sister has been in and out of love so many times that I can't keep track." He stopped at a stop sign and looked over at me. "How about you, Jill? Have you ever been in love?"

What a loaded question! I didn't want to lie, but I sure couldn't say that I was in love with him and had been for quite a while. "Don't you think I'm capable of loving someone? Do you think I sit at home and write about love without knowing what it's like?"

"How's your book coming?" Ben certainly changed the subject fast!

We talked about my book and about his farming. And we talked about you, Elizabeth, and how well your career is going. We both agreed we'd go to your next concert, no matter what.

At McDonald's we each ordered a Big Mac, large fries, and large Coke. I dropped a glob of that special sauce on my blouse and felt like a jerk. When I came out of the ladies' room, Bob Phillips was sitting with Ben and talking about corn and oats and cattle. Would you believe he stayed there!

Several days later Ben called and said that he had two tickets to the Don Francisco concert, and would I like to go with him. I agreed before he finished speaking. I wonder if he noticed that I was eager?

The concert was superb! I bought a tape and I'll share it with you this summer when you come home.

Ben walked me to my door and then started to peck

me on the cheek as if I were his sister, but I turned my head and our lips met. To me it was like an injection of lightning. He tensed, then he slipped his arms around me and really kissed me. I didn't want him to quit. I felt at home in his arms and I clung to him. He dropped his arms and I was forced to drop mine. He just looked at me, then rushed to his car and drove away.

I walked inside and leaned against the door, my eyes closed and my mouth tingling. What was Ben thinking now? Would he ever speak to me again?

Twice during the following week I almost walked down to see Ben, then stopped myself. Rejection was one experience I couldn't take, especially from Ben. Not knowing what he was thinking was better because I could always tell myself that he suddenly fell in love with me but couldn't believe it and needed time to think.

The next time I saw him was in town when I was walking out of the drugstore and he was just ready to walk in. I bumped into him. Literally! My face flamed and every part of me that touched him was on fire. I swallowed hard and eased away from him. "Excuse me. I don't usually run folks down."

"Hi, Jill." He just looked at me and tiny shivers ran up and down my back.

"Hi, Ben." I moved aside to let a man out of the store. "I've missed you."

"You have?" He missed me!

"I thought you'd be down to visit." He looked down, then right at me. His face was almost as red as his hair. "I hope my kiss didn't scare you away from me. I . . . I don't know what happened."

Didn't he ever read any romance books or watch a love story on TV? "Maybe you were using me as a stand-in for Christy Long."

He shook his head. "I knew it was you."

He'd kissed me!

He caught my hand—the one that didn't have my purse and paper bag. "Don't be frightened away by that kiss. We're friends. I want us always to be friends."

Friends? I jerked away from him and rushed away, tears filling my eyes. I never wanted to see him or talk to him again!

And when I reached my car I had a parking ticket on the windshield! I jerked it off and almost ripped it in half. When I looked up, Ben was standing beside me.

"You made me get a ticket with that talk about kissing!" I cried, shaking the ticket at him.

He caught my hand and pulled the ticket out of my fingers. "I'll pay for it."

"Why should you? Is that what friends do?"

"Why are you angry? Aren't we friends?"

Oh, I wanted to scream! And cry! But mostly I wanted to have him hold me tight and tell me that he loved me. I looked away from him.

"Jill, I bought that small farm next to us where Brian and Lisa Parr once lived. I'd like you to come look at the house with me to see if it has any possibilities. If it does, I'm going to move in. It's time I had a place of my own."

That could only mean one thing. He had marriage plans! I certainly wasn't going to look at the future Mrs. Ben Johnson's love nest! "I'm busy, Ben. Ask

Susan to go with you. Your own sister should be of more help than I could." Tears stung the corners of my eyes, but I didn't want Ben to see. I reached to unlock my car door, but Ben clamped his large hand over mine. I'm tall, but he seemed to tower over me as he stepped closer.

"I don't want Susan to look at the house. I want you to."

I wanted to look up and challenge him, but I was afraid he'd see the tears. I shrugged as if it really didn't matter and said, "I'll look at it with you. When did you have in mind?"

"Right now. I'll follow you home, then pick you up and take you there." He sounded as if he didn't want any argument, so I agreed.

All the way home I cried. I'm surprised I didn't go into the ditch. At home I called in to tell Mom that I was going with Ben, then slipped into his car, hugging the door. But he didn't seem to notice. He didn't look at me or talk to me until we stopped outside the small house. Since the Bradens had moved out, the house had been painted. It blended in beautifully with the trees around. A sharp pain of jealousy almost knocked me over. I didn't want some woman living in that adorable house with Ben.

"All right. I've seen it and I want to go." I was ready to burst into tears and I practically squeezed the blood out of my hands.

"We're going to look inside," said Ben as he jerked open his door.

I sat still and he jerked my door open and grabbed my arm and pulled me out.

I don't know what came over our mild-mannered

Ben. But I could tell he meant business.

He unlocked the door and I would have fled if I could have. He pushed open the door and I walked in with him so close behind I could feel his body heat. His breath stirred my hair as he said, "We are going to look at the whole house."

"That shouldn't take more than five seconds," I muttered.

He took a deep breath. "I know it's small. I hope it won't matter."

It wouldn't matter to me. The closer the better as far as I was concerned, but I didn't want any other woman this close to Ben.

The kitchen was a cheery yellow with yellow and white curtains at the window. My, but it would be fun to cook meals for Ben and me in that cute kitchen!

"The living room is only big enough for a couch, chair, coffee table and TV, but we won't need more than that."

We? He did have someone in mind. But who? Why did he suddenly look so hesitant? How dare he force me to give my opinion!

"There are two other rooms beside the bathroom. One could be a bedroom and the other a study."

My stomach tightened and I just could not move. Ben's hand tightened on my arm, but I pulled and almost broke his hold.

"Jill, do you hate it that much that you can't look at the other rooms? What is so bad about this place? Do you expect a mansion?"

I lifted my eyes to his and I didn't care if he saw the tears that burned my eyes. "How can you do this to me? I can't go into that bedroom!"

He sighed and stabbed his fingers through his red hair. "At least look in the other room. Is there room for a desk and file cabinet and typing table? Would it be too cramped?"

"It depends on how particular the girl is."

"How particular are you?"

I jerked away from him and stood there with my fists clenched at my sides. "I'm too particular to stay in this house that I love and know that you'll be living here with some girl that I'll hate!"

He got a funny look on his face. "What are you talking about?"

"Don't play games with me! You want me to look at this house so that you can feel good about asking some girl if she'll marry you and live here with you. I can't act cool and calm and tell you to bring that girl here to this little dream house. I can't!"

He reached for me, but I backed away until I was pressed against a wall that was painted a nice shade of blue. He cupped my face with his hand and I dropped my gaze.

"Look at me, Jill."

I couldn't.

He pressed his cheek against mine and I thought my heartbeats would deafen him.

"Please let me go," I said hoarsely.

"I can't! I can't."

My stomach fluttered and I slowly lifted my hand and buried my fingers in his hair that almost touched his collar. He trembled and slipped his arms around me.

"Jill, if someone asked you to marry him, would you?"

I bit the inside of my bottom lip.

Finally he lifted his head and looked at me. Our eyes locked and I could barely breathe.

"Who would ask me?"

A muscle jumped in his jaw. "I would."

"Then I'd say yes." Was this another one of my fantasies?

"You would?" He sounded surprised and I couldn't believe him.

"I love you," I whispered.

He kissed me then and it was better than anything I'd ever dreamed of. I kissed him back with a hunger that surprised even me.

After a long time he held me away. He looked boyishly young in his happiness. "I love you, Jill. But I didn't think you cared at all about me. You have said often that you wouldn't marry. You have said over and over that you are going to be a writer and maybe some year far away you'd get married."

"I am so sorry. I did mean it when I said it, but that was a long time ago. You changed my mind. I can't live without you. I can barely write."

"And do you think you could write here? Can you set your typewriter in here and write books?"

I slipped my arms around his neck again and moved close. He kissed me and I kissed him and I think he knew what I thought about that.

Finally we walked to the front room again and we stood arm in arm, looking around at our home.

"I'd like to move in right away," Ben said. "How soon can you be ready? Our families will want a grand wedding in the church with all of our friends, but I want a quiet one."

*I thought of all my daydreams about my wedding,
but I didn't care. I would stand in my living room in
front of the fireplace and get married if that's what
Ben wanted. "Anything you say is fine with me."*

*He grinned and sighed. "I think you'd really like a
big church wedding with Elizabeth and April and
May standing up with you, wouldn't you?"*

I wrinkled my nose and said, "Yes, I would."

*"Then we'll do it that way, but it will be soon. I'm
tired of being alone."*

*I went into his arms again and it was a long time
before we left the little house which would soon be our
home.*

*Elizabeth, will you be my maid of honor? We ordered
the invitations and will have them tomorrow. Our
wedding day is June 24. June 24! The beginning of
my life!*

*Won't it be wonderful to be not only best friends, but
sisters? I hope you're as happy about this as I am. I
can't wait to see you and talk to you. I think you'll love
our little house.*

Be happy for me, Libby.

*I told Susan a while ago. Of course I didn't go into
detail with her. She started crying, then hugged me
and ran to her room.*

*Our parents are thrilled about the marriage and
that we'll be living so close.*

*I was glad to hear about your agent. Is he young and
cute? Is he single? You have to get married someday,
Elizabeth.*

See you soon. I praise God daily for our friendship.

Love,
Jill (Johnson)

Elizabeth sniffed and brushed tears away as she pressed the letter to her heart. This was by far the best news yet, next to signing the contract with Marv Secord.

Trust Jill to think of Marv as a prospective husband. She'd be disappointed when she learned of his wife and baby daughter.

Slowly Elizabeth folded the pages together and pushed the letter back into the envelope. Ben and Jill. Adam and April. Joe and May. Would it ever be 'Elizabeth and Jerry'? And who would Susan marry? Would she marry this Sam Bouchard that Mom had said she had dated twice?

Just then Tammy knocked and poked her head in the door. "Ready to go, Libby?"

"Ready." Elizabeth looked around the bare room, then followed Tammy down the hall and the stairs and outdoors.

The late afternoon sun had lost most of its warmth and Elizabeth stood with the sun on her back, looking at Maddox School of Music.

This was the end of one part of her life, and the beginning of another. Suddenly she laughed and ran to Tammy's car.

SEVEN
Old friends

Elizabeth walked slowly into the church that she'd attended since coming to live with the Johnson family. Several people greeted her and she felt loved. How many of them remembered her first day? She'd sat in Sunday school with Susan and listened to Connie Tol teach. Then they'd walked to the sanctuary and she'd tried to sit beside Ben. Brenda Wilkens had wanted to sit beside Ben and she had absolutely insisted. Elizabeth had pinched the back of her leg behind her knee and Brenda had cried out in pain. Every eye had turned to them and Elizabeth had wanted to fade into the carpet. She'd moved over and sat with Susan.

That had been a long time ago. Today she wouldn't do such a thing. Would she? She grinned and walked with Tammy to the Sunday school wing. She reached the door, then stopped, her heart in her mouth. Jerry Grosbeck stood there dressed in a light gray suit and white shirt with a dark gray tie. His eyes darkened as he looked at her and she wondered desperately what he was thinking.

"Hello, Elizabeth," he said calmly as if he'd just seen her yesterday.

"Hello." The word barely came out. She wanted to call Tammy back, but she was walking into the classroom with Ben and Jill.

"It's been a long time."

"Yes, it has." She could smell his after-shave lotion and it was as foreign on him as the maturity that he wore as easily as the suit.

"You're looking good."

She glanced down at her white and pink dress and was glad that she was wearing it just now.

"Chuck told me about your agent. I'm happy for you. You're getting everything you ever wanted."

Not everything. She managed to smile. "I'm happy for you, too. Dad says you're a wonderful partner."

"We'd better get into class." He motioned for her to precede him and with all her willpower, she did.

She sat beside Susan just as Lane Becket started class. Jerry sat by himself on the far side of the room.

As Lane Becket prayed, Elizabeth tried to calm herself, and finally after whispering a prayer she felt better.

As Lane taught the lesson Elizabeth tried to sit still and not fidget with her Bible or purse. Susan frowned at her a couple of times, but she shrugged and Susan looked away.

Elizabeth bit the inside of her lip and tried to listen to Lane, but her thoughts returned to Jerry over and over.

How could she be calm around Jerry? She'd probably be in such turmoil that she wouldn't be able to play the piano. And how could she perform at Kramer

Auditorium next month with Jerry around?

And then her mind picked up something Lane had said, and she gripped her Bible and listened intently.

"Since Romans 8:37 says that we are more than conquerors through Christ, then we must act like it!" Lane grinned and leaned on the podium, his brown eyes twinkling. "Have you noticed that your mind often gets in the way of your actions? Your mind convinces you that you're a failure, that you can't accomplish what you want to.

"Romans 8:37 says that we are more than conquerors through Christ. It has to be so!

"But how do you get your mind to agree with that?"

Elizabeth waited, her eyes wide. She wanted to hear and know.

Lane flipped the pages of his Bible. "Look in 2 Corinthians 10:5. It says, 'Casting down imaginations, and every high thing that exalteth itself against the knowledge of God, and bringing into captivity every thought to the obedience of Christ.'"

Elizabeth felt as if she was sitting on the edge of her chair. She could feel others listening intently.

Lane stood up tall. "You must cast down your imaginations and your thoughts! You must tell yourself that God's Word is true no matter what your mind tries to tell you. Your mind shouldn't rule you. God's Word should!

"You are more than conquerors through Christ! That's the truth, the absolute truth, because it is God's Word.

"When a negative thought comes to you, refuse to think it. If you think it, and say it, you'll begin to believe it over God's Word. That shouldn't be.

"You are a new creature in Christ and God's ability and strength is in you. You are an overcomer in this life! YOU are more than a conqueror!"

The words rang inside Elizabeth and she suddenly felt strong and powerful and able to handle any situation.

She wasn't a failure, and never would be! She would play her concert in Kramer Auditorium, and she'd play well!

She glanced at Jerry. She would be able to talk with Jerry and be in the wedding with him if that's how it worked out, and she'd never have to hide from him or avoid him.

Just as class was over Susan turned to Elizabeth and said, "I must talk to you this afternoon! It can't wait!"

Elizabeth was puzzled by the intensity in Susan's voice and the look in her blue eyes. "All right. Anytime is fine with me."

"We'll go for a walk after dinner where we can be alone without any interruptions."

"It sounds very serious."

Susan flushed, then her face turned almost white. "It is," she whispered urgently.

Before Elizabeth could ask what it was about, Susan hurried away, her yellow skirt swirling around her pretty legs. Her red-gold hair hung almost to her narrow waist, and it bounced as she walked.

Later, after dinner, Elizabeth changed into jeans and a knit shirt and walked into the family room to find Susan. She found Ben and Jill instead.

Ben turned from kissing Jill and smiled at Elizabeth. "Let's go look at our house now. We want you to see what we've done to it."

"I'm waiting for Susan."

"She's on the phone in the study, and you know Susan and the phone. Tell Mom to tell Susan that you'll be back soon." Ben caught Elizabeth's hand and tugged her with him.

Jill laughed. "We won't take no for an answer, Elizabeth. You have to come with us."

Elizabeth shrugged with a laugh. "I'm outnumbered. But I wanted to see your house anyway." She had never seen Ben or Jill so happy. And when she'd seen Adam and April and Joe and May, she'd thought the same thing. Love was a mighty force!

Had her love for Jerry ever been that strong?

She frowned as she walked out of the house behind Jill. Why should she think about that now? Of course it was strong. She loved Jerry and she always would. He had been a part of her life since she was very young. He would always be a part of her life.

Elizabeth stopped in the driveway and looked back at the house. "I should see if Tammy wants to go with us."

Ben shook his head. "I heard her making arrangements with Toby to go riding."

"She said she wanted to ride a horse while she was here. Toby will be a good teacher." Elizabeth walked beside Jill down the drive. Snowball nickered in the pen beside the barn.

"Did you know Toby was accepted at State?" asked Ben.

"That's great!" Elizabeth sighed. "We're all growing

up. It's hard to imagine Toby going to college."

"He wants to be a history teacher," said Jill. "He'll be a natural. I don't think there is anything he doesn't know about history. I have to look up everything I want to know."

"He's a great kid," said Ben as he walked beside Jill, swinging their hands back and forth.

Elizabeth thought about the family as they walked down the side of the road in the warm summer sun. Ben was a farmer and he was going to marry Jill, a writer. Susan worked as a typist in Acme Factory in town. Who would she marry, and when? Kevin was studying to be a detective and he occasionally dated Cindy Beecher. And Toby was going to be a history teacher. He liked several girls, but none of them seriously.

Elizabeth brushed a fly off her arm. She was a concert pianist. And she wasn't going with anyone, nor did she have any plans for marriage.

Would the three weddings this summer make her feel bad?

April had driven out yesterday to tell her of their plans. "Adam came to see me and he just said right out that he loved me and wanted to marry me. I flew into his arms, of course, and almost knocked him over. Then we learned that Joe and May were getting married June 10, so we are, too. And, Elizabeth, you are going to be our maid of honor. It's going to be the most beautiful wedding in the world! And we'll be the happiest people!"

Elizabeth had looked at April and agreed, then later when she'd talked to the others she had believed in their happiness even more.

"We're here, Elizabeth," said Ben, shaking her arm. "I don't know where you are."

She grinned sheepishly. "Sorry." She looked at the house where she'd come often to baby-sit with Amy Parr. "I like it! It's so cozy, so cute! You could write a story about it, Jill."

Jill pressed her cheek against Ben's shoulder. "I already have. Ben and Jill fell in love and got married. They moved into the little dream house and lived happily ever after."

"That's a very good story," said Ben. He pulled a key from the pocket of his jeans. "Now, let's look inside."

Elizabeth walked through the house, exclaiming over this and that and turning away as Ben kissed Jill over the least little thing.

They stopped in the front room and Elizabeth sat on a blue flowered chair that she recognized had once been Vera's while Ben and Jill sat on the blue sofa. "This is very nice," said Elizabeth sincerely.

"We looked at the house that Joe is buying for him and May," said Ben. "It's a nice little house, too. It's in town, but they don't seem to care."

"Adam and April will live just down the road," said Jill. "It'll be fun to get together with them and have cookouts and sleigh rides and everything."

The thought of herself and Jerry living in a small house flashed into Elizabeth's mind and she immediately rejected it. She couldn't picture herself in a small house with Jerry. She would be traveling constantly, never in one city for very long. That was a true picture, and strangely enough Jerry didn't fit in it at all. She wanted to think on it more and puzzle it out, but Ben and Jill started talking about wedding plans and she had to listen and give her opinion.

Just then a car door slammed, then another. By the time Ben reached the door, someone knocked.

"Our first company," said Jill with a laugh and she and Elizabeth stood up. "Oh, this is exciting!"

Elizabeth looked at the two men at the door, then she cried out in surprise and delight. "Mark McCall! Nolen Brown! Jill, you remember our friends from Nebraska."

Jill nodded and Ben introduced them while Elizabeth just stood there looking at Mark and Nolen. They were both dressed in jeans and Western-cut multicolored shirts. Mark was about six inches taller than Nolen, and stronger looking. Nolen had a mustache that he hadn't had three years ago when the family had gone to Nebraska for Old Zeb's funeral.

"This is really a surprise," said Elizabeth with her hands on her waist.

"Your mother told us you were here," said Mark.

"We came to kiss the bride," said Nolen, his hazel eyes twinkling.

Elizabeth remembered how sullen and angry he'd been when he'd first moved to the Sandhill Ranch. He'd found love from others and from God, and it showed.

"I won't be a bride for a few weeks," said Jill.

Nolen shrugged with a grin. "I'll kiss you now, and again then. I don't mind."

"Can you stay for the wedding?" asked Ben as he brought chairs from the kitchen for them to sit on.

"I wish we could," said Mark. "But we're only here a few days. You know how busy life on the ranch is. We came to check on a quarterhorse stallion near here."

Elizabeth listened as Mark and Nolen talked about the ranch and she once again was amazed that part of Sandhill Ranch was hers. Old Zeb had given it to Frank Dobbs, her real dad, and he'd given it to her. Three years ago when Old Zeb had died, he'd willed his part of the property to Nolen.

Mark told about their cousin Holly's wedding, and that his sister Shauna was expecting a baby soon. She was enjoying living in town and being married to a high school English teacher.

"Tell me again who is who," said Jill with a slight frown.

"It is a little hard to follow," said Nolen. He counted on his fingers as he talked. "Mark, Shauna, and Vickie McCall are brother and sisters. Holly and Aaron Davis are brother and sister. I, Nolen Brown, am an only child, and we're all cousins and we all live in Nebraska."

"What's happening with Aaron?" asked Ben.

"He's studying electronics in college and Vickie has one more year of high school. She said to tell Kevin and Toby a special hello from her," said Mark with a chuckle.

Ben turned to Jill and laughed also. "Vickie used to run after Kevin and Toby and kiss them when they were all little and the boys hated it."

"Now, all the boys are chasing Vickie," said Nolen, lifting his dark brows.

They locked up the house and drove back to Johnsons. When they walked into the family room, Susan and Tammy were watching TV and Vera and Chuck were reading. Susan jumped up and gripped Elizabeth's arm.

While Ben introduced Tammy to Mark and Nolen, Susan whispered fiercely, "You said we'd go for a walk and talk."

"I'm sorry. I forgot. We can talk later. OK?" Elizabeth looked at her arm. It was red where Susan had gripped her. What was bothering Susan?

"Hey, Elizabeth," said Nolen as he looked from Tammy to Elizabeth. "Has anyone told you that you look like twins?"

"A few people have," said Elizabeth dryly.

"I'm better looking," said Tammy, giggling.

"But I play the piano better," said Elizabeth, laughing with Tammy.

"You both look like winners to me," said Mark as he slipped an arm around each girl. "How does this place rate two of you? I would've thought one would be plenty."

"We'll take one home to Nebraska with us," said Nolen.

They laughed and joked and Elizabeth looked at Susan and the smile died on her face. Susan looked ready to burst into tears.

Elizabeth stepped toward Susan, but she turned and hurried from the room. Elizabeth started to follow, but Mark spoke to her, then Nolen asked if she still played the piano. She frowned at him, then realized that he was only teasing.

"We are all set for a private concert," said Mark as he sat on the end of the couch with Tammy and Nolen beside him.

Elizabeth thought about Susan, then looked at the piano. She'd talk to Susan later. Right now she had a concert to give.

She sat at the piano and touched her fingers to the keys.

EIGHT
Double wedding

Elizabeth stood beside the pen and stroked
Snowball's face, but her mind wasn't on the white
mare. It was on the day almost two years ago when
she'd forced Jerry to say good-bye to her. She could
tell that he held no bitterness or anger toward her,
but neither did he seem to love her still. He talked
with her when he was around, but he never went out
of his way to be with her. Now that Mark and Nolen
and Tammy were gone, Jerry might spend more time
with her.

Elizabeth sighed and looked up at the sky. It looked
as if it would rain. Just so it didn't rain Saturday
morning for April and May's wedding.

My, but the gowns were beautiful! Elizabeth leaned
against the top rail with a dreamy expression. It had
been fun shopping with April and May, for identical
white gowns with long trains and lots of lace. Elizabeth's long dress was green with a lighter green sash
and hat. Susan's gown was light green with a shade
darker sash and hat. They were each going to carry

one long-stemmed white rose. Jerry and Ben would be groomsmen. She couldn't picture herself walking down the aisle toward Jerry. Each time she thought of it, she'd seen herself walking toward Ben, and Susan walking toward Jerry.

How very foolish! Why even think about it?

She turned to walk toward the house, then stopped at the sight of Jerry's white and blue Mustang driving up the long driveway. A warm wind blew the swing in the front yard back and forth. The rustling of the trees sounded almost as loud as the chickens clucking in the chicken pen. Goosy Poosy honked and waddled toward the car, then turned and waddled back as if he'd lost interest once he recognized the car.

Elizabeth rubbed her hands on her shorts, then waited for Jerry who was walking purposefully toward her. He was dressed in dark blue shorts and a white terry shirt.

For a minute she thought of running away to hide, then realized there was no need. She didn't feel upset or frightened or embarrassed. "Hi, Jerry. Isn't this a beautiful day?" She smiled and was glad to see he did, too.

"Aren't you glad you're here right now instead of in the city where it is hot?" Jerry leaned against the fence, one foot on the bottom rail, his head turned to her.

"You spend a lot of time here, don't you, Jerry?"

She saw him stiffen, then he just shrugged. "I like it here. It's very restful. And cooler than my place."

"I hear you have an apartment not too far from Dad's store."

"That's right. It's small, but it makes me feel very independent. I see my foster parents often." He sighed and looked across the yard. "We have it good, Libby. You and I do. I see little kids everyday who are mistreated and unloved. I see us the way we were about ten years ago. Only these kids don't have loving parents, like the Johnsons and the McAlveys. They have foster homes without Christ and without love. I'd like to take them home with me, every one of them."

"When you get married, then you'll be able to." Now, why had she said anything about marriage? She glanced quickly at him, but he didn't seem to notice what she'd said.

He stood quietly for a long time. Lightning flashed across the sky and he looked up, then at Elizabeth. "I need a favor, Libby."

"Call me Elizabeth, and I'll do anything," she said with a grin.

He lifted his brows, then looked serious again. "I need you to talk to Susan."

"I've been trying to! I know there is something important on her mind, but she works days, then each evening we've been helping the twins. There hasn't been time."

Jerry thoughtfully rubbed his jaw. "I wish she wouldn't go with that Sam Bouchard." Jerry caught Elizabeth's hand and held it firmly. "You could talk to Susan and make her understand. That man is too old for her. Too old! He's thirty and she's twenty-one. I don't like it at all!"

Elizabeth looked at their hands and didn't feel a thing. How strange. She smiled at him and loved him for his concern for Susan. He was a dear, dear man.

Any girl would be proud to be his wife. But she wasn't to be his wife. She knew it as clearly as if God had written it across the sky.

"Will you see what you can do, Elizabeth?"

The back door slammed and she looked to see Susan standing there, but before she could move Susan rushed back in the house. "I'll do what I can, Jerry, I promise. But if she loves this Sam Bouchard, then I can't do a thing."

Jerry frowned and turned once again to lean on the fence. "She doesn't love him! He's not right for her. She wants a life like Vera's. Sam would have her working in his business, and going off in all directions. No, Susan wouldn't like that life at all."

"Why don't we go to the house right now? I'll talk to Susan and you can do whatever you came to do." She suddenly realized she didn't know why he was there. Had he finally come to see her?

"I like it here. Susan and I usually watch TV or talk or play games together. But since you're going to talk to Susan, I'll find someone else to talk to."

Elizabeth walked toward the house with Jerry beside her and she realized that she felt very comfortable beside him. He was like Ben—easy to be with.

She stopped him at the picnic table, her hand on his arm. "Jerry, I need to say something. Do you mind?"

He cupped her face with his large hand and she leaned her head into his hand. "Say away, Libby."

"You are a precious man, and I love you." He didn't say anything and she caught his hand in hers and held it. "But, Jerry, I love you the way I love Ben. I should have realized it sooner, but I didn't. I thought I was dying of love for you. And in a way I was, because you are a part of my past. We are linked together in a special way. We'll always be. I want to be free to love you this way. Can I be?"

He bent forward and kissed her cheek. "Yes, my Libby. It took me a long time to realize that I loved you in a special way, but not as a husband loves a wife. I wanted to tell you, but I couldn't bring myself to open the subject."

"Oh, Jerry." Tears stung her eyes as she slipped her arms around him and hugged him. His arms tightened around her and they stood together for a while, then Elizabeth stepped away. "I was so afraid! But then I knew I had nothing to fear. You are Jerry Grosbeck. You have your life that you must lead the way God planned, and I have my life that I must lead the way God planned. I almost saw this several days ago, but it escaped me. Now, it's very clear. You couldn't drop your life and come follow after me on my career. And I could never give up my concerts to stay here with you. I have been so slow!"

"It doesn't do any good to have hindsight. We'll look ahead and go from there." He opened the back door and held it for her. "You won't forget to talk to Susan, will you?"

"Talk to me about what?" asked Susan coldly from where she stood just inside the hall off the porch.

Elizabeth looked quickly at Jerry and saw him flush. "I always talk to Susan. We're sisters." Elizabeth turned to Susan whose face was pale. "Hello, Susan. How are you? What's new?" Oh, she was talking too much! Why couldn't she close her mouth?

"I'm going out, so please excuse me." Susan flipped her hair over her shoulder and started past, but Jerry caught her arm. She looked down at his hand, then way up at him. She didn't reach even his chin. "Let me go."

"I thought we were going to spend the evening together since you don't have to be gone with April and May."

"I'm going for a ride with Sam Bouchard. I'll see you Saturday at the wedding."

Jerry reluctantly dropped his hand and Susan walked away. Elizabeth looked after Susan with a frown.

"I have never seen her this upset," Elizabeth said as she walked with Jerry to the family room. "It makes me feel terrible! I suddenly realize how totally happy I am, but Susan is totally miserable."

Jerry started to sit on Chuck's chair, then walked to the fireplace and stood in front of the empty grate, his hands locked behind his back. "I'd like to tell that Sam Bouchard to keep away from Susan!"

Elizabeth sat on the arm of the couch and studied Jerry thoughtfully. "Aren't you being a little overprotective?"

"She needs protecting! She needs someone special in her life!"

"Just how do you feel about Susan?"

"Me?" Jerry strode to the window and looked out, then turned around. "She's very special to me. I don't know!"

Elizabeth tipped her head thoughtfully. "Do you . . . love her?"

"Of course I love her! Who wouldn't?" He ran his fingers through his dark hair, then fingered the scar on the side of his face.

"No, Jerry. I mean the way a man loves a woman. The way a husband loves a wife." Elizabeth stood up slowly and watched the expressions cross Jerry's face.

"What a thing to ask me! Susan is . . . Susan. I am Jerry Grosbeck, the foster kid with a scar."

"You are a wonderful man who is full of love and who has a successful future. So what if you were an aid kid? So what if you have a scar?" She stepped toward him, her hands on her hips. "Look at me! I am a concert pianist! The skinny little tough kid with the mouth like a sewer!"

He ran his finger around his collar and his face looked on fire. "What are you trying to tell me, Libby?"

"Nothing, Jerry. I just think you should look at your feelings for Susan, then go from there."

His face turned as white as his scar and he rushed from the room. Elizabeth stood very still until she heard the back door slam. Did Jerry love Susan? And what were Susan's feelings for Jerry?

The phone rang and Elizabeth jumped, then laughed under her breath as she reached to answer it.

It was April and she sounded rushed as usual. "Elizabeth, is it all right if you stand with Ben, and Susan with Jerry at the wedding? Joe said he'd rather have it that way, and the rest of us don't care."

"It's fine with me, April. I'll see you for practice tomorrow, then the wedding Saturday morning."

Elizabeth forced herself to remain calm on Saturday as she waited for her turn to walk down the long aisle to the front of the church where the pastor was waiting.

Susan reached the mark that was the sign for Elizabeth to start. She took a deep breath and slowly walked toward the front of the church. From the corner of her eye she could see friends and she could hear soft whispers. She knew they were saying that Susan was absolutely beautiful, but could they say that about her? She felt beautiful, but her mirror showed her a tall, thin girl with a plain face and ordinary brown hair that was curled.

She looked at Ben and he smiled, then she looked at Jerry, but he was looking at Susan. Did Jerry have his feelings sorted out yet?

She took her place and the music swelled to let everyone know that the brides were coming—first May, then April. As May reached the front row of seats Joe stepped forward and Chris Allison handed May to Joe. As Chris walked back for April, Joe and May stepped into place near the minister. Elizabeth shivered excitedly and hoped the rose wasn't shaking hard enough to drop its petals.

Someone sniffed loudly and Elizabeth thought it was Jean Allison as she realized how empty their house would be without the twins. Even when the twins shared an apartment they'd made sure they stayed often with their foster parents.

Adam's face practically glowed as he reached for April and led her into place.

Elizabeth listened intently as the couples exchanged vows that they'd written themselves. The beauty of their promises to each other brought tears to her eyes. She glanced at Susan and she was blinking away tears, too.

After the prayer the minister introduced the couples proudly. Adam lifted April's veil and kissed her while

Joe lifted May's veil and kissed her. Then they smiled at their friends and rushed down the aisle as the organ played. Ben nodded and Elizabeth walked toward him, meeting him in the center, then they rushed after the bridal couples. Elizabeth knew Jerry and Susan were right behind and she wished that she knew what they were thinking and feeling.

She squeezed Ben's arm and smiled at him. With her heels, she was almost as tall as Ben. He looked very handsome in his cream tux and shirt. Was Jill looking with longing and love at Ben right now as they stopped in the receiving line in the church foyer?

Ben leaned down with his mouth close to Elizabeth's ear. "Toby and Kevin are taking care of the cars. They found several friends to help them. Everybody will know that there has been a wedding!" He laughed softly and Elizabeth joined in.

Her hand ached and her face felt as if it would crack by the time all the people had passed through the line. She needed a drink of punch and a comfortable chair to collapse into.

"Tired?" asked Jerry.

She nodded and leaned momentarily against him. "Are you?"

"Not a bit!" he teased. Then he laughed. "I am, and I think Susan is, too. How about it, Susan?"

She nodded and Elizabeth could see the strain on her face. "I hope no one is offended, but I must leave right after the pictures are taken."

"I'll drive you home," said Jerry, sounding very concerned as he bent over her.

She moved back. "No! I'm sure Elizabeth wants you

to drive her home. The two of you have a lot of talking and planning to do."

"Not a lot, but some," said Elizabeth as she realized that in a few days Ben and Jill would be getting married and she and Jerry would be standing up for them.

Elizabeth laughed softly. "Oh, but I love weddings!"

NINE
News about Tammy

Elizabeth frowned as she watched Susan drive onto the road to town to meet Sam Bouchard. Since the wedding Saturday she'd been trying to talk to Susan, but it seemed as if Susan was avoiding her. But why would she?

Goosy Poosy rubbed his long neck up and down Elizabeth's bare leg and she stroked the goose absently.

"Now, that is something you don't normally see."

She turned and laughed as Chuck stopped beside her. "Hi, Dad."

"Goosy Poosy usually leaves you alone." Chuck bent to rub the goose's neck. "You go lie down under the lilac bush and cool off, Goosy Poosy."

The goose honked, then half ran, half walked to the lilac bush as Chuck slipped his arm around Elizabeth's waist.

"It's good to have you home, honey. In a few days Ben will be married and gone, then you'll be on your concert tour. In the fall Kevin and Toby will be away again, and maybe Susan." Chuck cleared his throat. "Things are changing, my girl. There are so many new beginnings."

"And all happy ones, Dad." She held his hand against her cheek.

He sighed. "Mom and I are sometimes lonely, but we're glad for the happiness around us. We're happy, too, but the house feels mighty empty, and will be even more so soon."

Elizabeth walked with Chuck to the picnic table and sat with him, her hand holding his firmly. "Dad, why don't you get more foster children?"

"Mom and I have talked about it, but we didn't think it was fair to you children. You'd have to give up your bedrooms."

She turned to him, her eyes glowing. "Oh, Dad, we only use our bedrooms occasionally. I wouldn't mind sleeping in the guest room when I do come home. And Ben won't need his room at all. That gives you two empty bedrooms right away!"

Chuck laughed and shook his head. "You're right. We'll pray about this."

"And maybe someone else will come into the family, someone in desperate need of love." Elizabeth blinked away tears and rubbed her nose. "Jerry knows a lot of kids who need a loving family."

Chuck nodded, then sat quietly for a long time. "You and Jerry are at peace, aren't you?"

"Yes, Dad." She told him about her feelings for Jerry, and he said he was glad.

"I've been watching love grow between Susan and Jerry this past year and it concerned me for your sake."

Elizabeth gasped, her eyes wide. "Do you think they are in love?"

"I thought so, and so did Vera. We thought after you came home you'd realize your love wasn't what you thought. And you did, but Jerry and Susan seem very far apart."

"Is Susan more interested in Sam Bouchard than you thought?"

Chuck shrugged. "Maybe so, maybe so. But she glows when Jerry's around. At least she did."

"I want to see Susan have a happy new beginning," said Elizabeth huskily. "I love her, and I want her to be as happy as the rest of us."

Just then a car drove in and parked outside the garage. Elizabeth jumped in surprise. "It's Tammy! And she didn't even call to say she was coming."

Tammy rushed toward Elizabeth, tears streaming down her face. "Oh, Libby, Libby!"

Chuck cleared his throat, his forehead puckered with concern. "Tammy, what's wrong? How can I help you?"

Tammy sniffed hard and tried to wipe away her tears as she shook her head. "I need to see Libby alone."

"I'll leave you girls alone, then." Chuck walked through the back door and Elizabeth stared at Tammy, her heart racing strangely.

"Shall we sit down out here or go inside?"

Tammy dropped her purse on the picnic table. "My mother came to see me again yesterday." Fresh tears gushed from Tammy's eyes. Her sundress looked rumpled.

"What did she say to upset you this much?" Elizabeth wanted to find Phyllis LaDere and tell her to leave Tammy alone from now on.

Tammy sniffed hard. "I said I wouldn't cry anymore. I said I wouldn't! And I won't. I'll sit down and we can talk." She pulled a tissue from her purse and blew her nose.

Elizabeth sank to the bench and stared at Tammy.

"I wasn't going to come, Libby, but I started driving this morning and before I knew it I was coming this way. So I said, why not, and here I am."

"Are you hungry? Thirsty?"

"I just need to talk to you. Oh, I hope I can do it! You have a right to know!"

"What?" Elizabeth gripped her hands together in her lap, and shivers ran up and down her spine. "Is it bad?"

Tammy brushed her hair back with a trembling hand. "Mother was so angry because I became a Christian. She said she didn't want me mixed up that way. I said I was happy for the first time in my life. She left and didn't bother me again until yesterday. She said she had a nice man for me, and that she wanted me to go home with her. She said the man had money and he might even want to marry me someday. I said no and she blew up. I thought she was going to hit me, but she said . . . she said. . . ."

"Yes? Go on." Elizabeth leaned forward, her eyes intently on Tammy.

"She said, 'Tammy, I raised you all these years and I deserve better than you're giving me. Your father couldn't marry me, but I kept you and I gave you a good home. I didn't treat you the way Marie treated Libby. I raised you. All I'm asking is one favor and you won't do it! I need money right now since Jack left me. Monty will take care of me as long as you're with him.'"

Tammy shuddered. "So I said, 'Why don't you find my father and ask him for money? He should help you.'

"She said, 'Ask your father? You crazy fool! Your father is dead! He died several years ago in Nebraska. Your father was Frank Dobbs. He was married to my sister Marie, but I gave birth to you and I raised you. He can't help me now.'

"And I fell apart, Libby. Frank Dobbs is my father, too! We're sisters!"

Elizabeth sagged against the table, her face pale and her body shaking. Frank Dobbs was the father of Tammy! Her father was Tammy's father!

Tammy rested her hand on Elizabeth's shoulder. "I told Mother that we both had a right to know, that we should've been told years ago."

"Does my mother know?"

"Yes. That's why they've hated each other all these years."

"Does Grandma LaDere know?"

"Yes."

Elizabeth locked her icy fingers together. "It's funny to have a picture of your father shattered. It took me years to forgive him for running out on me, then he sent me the puzzle box and said he wanted to get acquainted, but he never once said he had another daughter. He kept the biggest secret of all! Then he died before I could see him and talk to him."

After a long time Tammy said, "We're sisters, Libby. And I'm glad!"

Elizabeth slowly turned and looked at Tammy, then reached for her and they sobbed together. Finally Elizabeth pulled away and laughed shakily. "I'm glad we're sisters. I'm not going to be ashamed of you because of my father. Let's go inside right now and tell my family."

Tammy hesitated then walked with Elizabeth.

Elizabeth stopped just inside the door with a grin. "We're sisters, so what's mine is yours. This family is your family now. I know they'll feel the same way."

Later on, Elizabeth sat on the piano bench, her back to the keyboard, smiling proudly as her family talked with Tammy, making her feel loved and wanted. Even Susan smiled and lost some of the anguish that showed on her face.

At bedtime Elizabeth called Tammy into her room and together they looked at the puzzle box and all the things inside that Frank Dobbs had sent years ago. They read the letters he'd written and cried again.

"I am going to share my Nebraska property with you, Tammy."

Tammy shook her head as she pulled her bathrobe around her slender body. "You can't do that. He wanted you to have it."

"I think he wanted us both to have it, but he couldn't say it without giving away the secret. And maybe he thought we'd both hate him forever if we knew the truth. I'll find out how to do it, then we'll both own part of Sandhill Ranch in Nebraska."

Tammy laughed, her head back and her blue eyes sparkling. "I'll enjoy that. I might even buy myself some cowboy boots and a hat!"

"And as soon as I have enough time between concerts and you can get off work, we'll visit our ranch together."

Tammy nodded. "Let's go tomorrow. I'd like to see Mark and Nolen again. I really like them."

"We'll marry them and settle in Nebraska and be rancher's wives!" Elizabeth laughed and Tammy joined in.

The door opened and Susan poked her head in, smiling slightly. "I heard all the laughing and wanted to hear what's funny so I can laugh, too."

"Come in," said Tammy.

"I just said that Tammy and I could go to Nebraska together and marry Mark and Nolen." She started to say more but Susan swayed and would have fallen, but Tammy caught her.

"What's wrong?" cried Elizabeth, immediately catching Susan's icy hands. "Are you sick?"

"I'll be all right." She took a deep breath and stood up, retying her bathrobe with shaky hands. Elizabeth suddenly realized how thin Susan had gotten. What was making her so unhappy that she couldn't eat?

"I didn't mean to break up your party," said Susan as she walked slowly to the door. "Good night. I'll see you both tomorrow."

"I don't think you should go to work in the morning," said Elizabeth in concern. "Stay in bed in the morning and I'll call in for you."

"You need to rest," said Tammy. "They can get along without you at work for one day, can't they?"

Susan nodded, then slowly walked out, closing the door behind her.

Elizabeth shook her head. "I feel so terrible! Everyone is happy except Susan."

Tammy cleared her throat. "Do you think she wants

to marry that guy she's going with, but he won't marry her?"

"I wish I knew," said Elizabeth thoughtfully, looking intently at the closed door. "I think tomorrow I will work at making Susan Johnson happy."

TEN
A happy beginning

Elizabeth looked up after finishing the sonata, then heard the family room door open behind her. She turned, expecting to see Jerry, who had said he'd be right over after she'd called. Instead, she saw Susan. She was dressed in jeans and a long-sleeved flowered blouse.

"I'm going riding for a while. I'll see you later."

Elizabeth jumped up in panic. Susan must not leave before Jerry came! "Why don't you grab a bite to eat first? You haven't been eating much at all lately."

Susan shook her head and the long braids hanging over her slender shoulders moved. "I'm really not hungry. I'll be back before lunch and then I'll eat."

"Do you want me to ride with you?"

"I need to be alone, but thanks anyway."

Oh, her plan was not going to work after all! "I guess I need to practice. Next week will be very hectic with Ben's wedding and I won't have much time to practice."

"You'll probably be making plans of your own, won't

you?" Susan's face was as white as the lamp shade beside her.

"Marv Secord makes the plans and I just follow them. He said that he'd get me into Grace Hall someday. That will be the ultimate!"

"What will Jerry do while you're traveling all around?"

Elizabeth looked closely at Susan, then shrugged. "He'll be here doing what he usually does. He might even decide to marry."

Susan locked her fingers together and Elizabeth saw the rise and fall of her chest. "Marry you?"

"Not me! I told you before that piano is my life. Can you see Jerry Grosbeck following me around the country? No. His life is right here." She pushed her hands into her pockets to hide their trembling as she decided that she'd go ahead with her plan. "He fits right in at the store with Dad. But he does need a wife. He wants to have a home and a family. I wouldn't be surprised if he some day takes in foster kids just like the Johnson family."

Susan swallowed hard. "Who would he marry?"

Elizabeth shrugged again. "I don't know if anyone would have him since he had such a terrible background and then there's that scar. . . ."

"Why should that matter? So what if he doesn't have an ordinary family? So what if he has a scar! Who ever notices?"

"Sometimes I think that he doesn't feel good enough to marry a nice girl with a good home."

Susan covered her face and burst into tears. Elizabeth drew her close and held her as if she were a child. Finally Susan pulled away and wiped her tears.

"Libby, I love him," she whispered hoarsely. "I have for a long, long time. But I thought you loved him and that you'd marry each other. I felt so terrible when he'd come over and I'd sit with him and pretend that he loved me and had come to see me instead of coming here because he missed you so much."

Elizabeth hugged Susan close. "Jerry loves me the way I love him. It just took us both a long time to realize our love was a brother-and-sister love, not a mad, passionate love where we couldn't live without each other."

Susan hugged her arms to her and hunched her shoulders. "I don't think I can live without him."

"And what about Sam Bouchard?"

"He knows that I love someone else, and that I go with him just to have something to do. He doesn't want to marry for a while, so he goes with me for companionship, too."

Elizabeth rubbed her finger across the lamp table. "Jerry told me to talk to you and convince you to stop seeing Sam. Jerry said Sam was the wrong man for you."

Susan's head shot up and her eyes widened. "And who does he think *is* the right man?"

"He didn't say."

"If he were here right now, I'd find out!" Susan clenched her fists at her sides and her eyes flashed. She looked like the old Susan, not the sad, tired one.

A door closed and Elizabeth's heart leaped. That had to be Jerry. Everyone had gone to town and wouldn't be back until after lunch. "And what would you say to him?"

"Plenty!"

Jerry stopped in the doorway. Susan gasped, and Elizabeth giggled under her breath.

"Come in, Jerry," said Elizabeth. "I'll go fix us a pitcher of iced tea."

"I'll help you," said Jerry, but Elizabeth shook her head.

"I can manage. Talk to Susan a while and I'll be back later." She turned at the door and looked back. Susan was engulfing Jerry with her large blue eyes and he was staring down at the floor. "I might even decide to stir up a coffee cake. Susan hasn't eaten breakfast yet."

"Take your time," said Susan, her eyes meeting Elizabeth's.

Elizabeth nodded as she realized Susan was saying to be gone as long as possible. Good for Susan!

Instead of walking to the kitchen, Elizabeth stood in the hall pressed against the wall outside the family room. She knew she shouldn't eavesdrop, but she couldn't help herself. She had to hear what Susan said. She had to know how Jerry responded! She stood very still and listened intently.

"Shall we sit down, Jerry?"

The springs of the couch moved. "Why aren't you at work, Susan? You aren't sick, are you?"

"Not anymore."

Elizabeth shivered and forced back a nervous giggle.

"Do you know why Elizabeth called me this morning and sounded as if my coming here was a matter of life and death?"

"Did she call you?" The couch moved again and when Susan spoke Elizabeth knew she was on the far side of the room. "I'm glad she did, Jerry. I want to talk to you." Her voice quivered. "I'm never going with Sam Bouchard again. I decided he's not the kind of man I want."

Elizabeth could hear Jerry stand up. "I'm glad, Susan. He's too old for you. He's not your type at all. You need a man who will love you and appreciate you for yourself."

"And do *you?*" Susan's voice was very low and Elizabeth could barely hear her.

"What?" asked Jerry in surprise.

Elizabeth almost forgot to breathe. How could she be so terrible as to stand and listen to this private conversation?

"Jerry, will you marry me?"

Elizabeth gasped, then clamped her hand over her mouth. Had they heard her?

"You don't know what you're saying, Susan. It's not funny to tease me that way."

"Am I teasing?" Susan laughed softly. "I thought I was totally serious. I love you and I want to marry you."

Elizabeth waited, then finally peeked in. Jerry and Susan were wrapped in each other's arms and kissing as if they'd never quit. Elizabeth smiled tearfully, then quickly ducked back.

"I'll marry you on one condition," Jerry said in a soft, teasing voice.

"And what is that?"

"That we get married soon."

"But we can't! Ben and Jill's wedding is next week. We're busy getting ready for that."

"I'll talk to Ben and see if we can have a double wedding. We aren't the Brakie twins, but we can still have a double wedding."

They were silent for a long time, then talked too softly for Elizabeth to hear. Finally Susan said, "Jerry, I would marry you tomorrow if you wanted me to. I can't live without you!"

"Oh, Susan! I never knew how much I loved you until a few days ago. Then I couldn't say anything because you seemed to care for that Sam Bouchard."

"Darling Jerry, you are my love and you always will be."

"I love you, Susan. I love you."

Elizabeth tiptoed to the kitchen and sat at the table, her hands over face. Love was too beautiful for words. Could piano take the place of love? Maybe she should give it up and find a man who loved her the way Jerry loved Susan.

But how could she quench the burning desire to be a famous concert pianist?

She lifted her head and looked unseeing at the plants hanging at the kitchen windows. God's plan for her life was to be a concert pianist. When the time was right for her, then she'd fall in love and marry. But it would be to a man who shared her goals.

She closed her eyes and folded her hands on the Bible that Chuck had laid on the table earlier. "Heavenly Father, you know me. You made me and you put this music inside me to share with others. Help me to do it, and do it well!"

Finally she opened the Bible to one of her favorite Psalms, the ninety-sixth, and read softly, "Oh, sing unto the Lord a new song: sing unto the Lord, all the earth. Sing unto the Lord, bless his name; show forth his salvation from day to day. Declare his glory among the heathen, his wonders among all people.

For the Lord is great, and greatly to be praised."

She smiled. She would play unto the Lord. She would play and she would bless the Lord and bless others.

"Where is the tea?"

She jumped up, grinning sheepishly at Jerry and Susan. "Sorry. I forgot to make it, but I will now."

"We're going to be married!" cried Susan, gripping Jerry's arm as if she'd never let it go.

"We called Jill and she said she'd love to have a double wedding with us," said Jerry.

Elizabeth kissed Susan, then Jerry. "Congratulations! I'm very happy for both of you. And Susan, I'm glad to see the sadness gone. I missed that bright, cheery girl who was always laughing with happiness."

"So did I," said Jerry. He kissed Susan and she glowed even more. "We must find a place to live."

"Your apartment will be just fine until we find what we want."

Elizabeth nodded. "The next few days will be full just getting you both ready. What a summer for weddings!"

"Maybe you'll be next, Elizabeth," said Susan, smiling.

Elizabeth shook her head. "Not yet, Susan. I have something else to do first. I have all this music inside me that must come out. Later, I'll have a home of my own and a man to love me."

On June 24 Elizabeth stood at the altar of the church in almost the same spot she had for the twins' wedding.

She looked down at the bouquet of bright yellow

roses with white daisies and baby's breath. Her hair was piled on top of her head and daisies were woven through it. She glanced at Tammy beside her and it was like looking in a mirror. They were dressed alike in soft yellow and carried identical bouquets.

Jerry and Ben were dressed in white tails with pleated shirts. The tuxes that Kevin and Toby wore were without tails and both boys looked very handsome and grown-up. Kevin smiled at Elizabeth and she smiled back.

Susan stood with her hand in Jerry's and said her vows in a clear, strong voice. She looked more beautiful than Elizabeth had ever seen her in the simple gown with the high neck and long sleeves. All she needed was a cameo at her throat to look as if she'd just stepped out of the 1800s. Even her hair was in a pompadour with daisies threaded through it.

Jerry spoke his vows and Elizabeth heard the fervency of his voice and knew he would keep the vows forever. She had heard both couples discuss their views that marriage was forever, and not to be dissolved in a divorce court.

Elizabeth watched Jill as she made her vows to Ben. She wore a veil over her brown curls and it blurred her face. Her dark eyes shone with love for Ben. Her dress was an empire style with a long train that later would be buttoned up into a bustle.

Ben's face turned slightly red as he made his promises to Jill. The little flower girls looked up at him and Elizabeth was afraid they'd burst out laughing. They had teased Ben at practice about forgetting his words.

Elizabeth bit the inside of her bottom lip as she

watched her little cousins. They didn't giggle and she was glad.

The minister prayed a blessing on the couples and they kissed, then hurried down the aisle. The flower girls followed them, then Elizabeth with Kevin and Tammy with Toby.

"I can't take another wedding this summer," Kevin whispered close to Elizabeth's ear as they stood in the receiving line.

She grinned and whispered back, "I don't think I could either. But if you decided to get married, I would come anyway."

"Not me! I am not getting married for years. I have some detective work to do first."

"And I have some piano playing to do first." Before she could say more, Uncle Luke caught her hand, then gave her a bear hug. He didn't look any older than he had when she'd first met him when she was twelve. He looked a little more like Chuck, though.

"We already bought tickets for your concert at Kramer Auditorium, Libby."

"I'm glad."

Aunt Gwen hugged her, then looked at her with a shake of her head. "Is this beautiful girl really my little Libby Dobbs?"

Elizabeth nodded as she remembered when Aunt Gwen was Miss Miller, her social worker. Many times Miss Miller had come to her rescue, but Elizabeth cringed to think how mean and foul-mouthed she'd been to her. "I'm so glad you could make it to the wedding. And your girls were such beautiful flower girls."

"They take after their mother," said Luke as he slipped his arm around Gwen.

"Let me shake hands with Libby," said Scottie as he held out his hand. He looked very grown-up in his blue suit and white shirt. His hair was still fine and silky and about the same shade as Susan's.

"Scottie, you just won't stop growing, will you?" asked Elizabeth as she kissed his cheek. She'd first met him when he was four. His mother had died, then Luke had married Gwen. "Are you really thirteen years old?"

Scottie nodded, then had to keep moving as someone else spoke to Elizabeth. It was Grandma and Grandpa Johnson who must have arrived while she was at the church.

"I was afraid you'd miss the wedding," she said as she hugged and kissed them.

"We almost did," said Grandpa with a twinkle in his eye. "I turned off on a road that I thought was a shortcut, but it wasn't."

"And he got lost," said Grandma, laughing softly. She was short like Susan and well rounded as a grandma should be. "But we made it. And you all look so beautiful! Two grandchildren getting married in one day is a treat."

"We are going to drive down for your concert next month, Elizabeth," said Grandpa. "We had to miss the others, but we refuse to miss this one!"

"I have tickets for you at home, so don't buy any." Elizabeth hugged them again and they walked on.

By midnight she finally crawled into bed. That had to be the last wedding for a long time!

"Elizabeth, are you asleep?"

She sat up. "Not yet, Dad."

He walked in and sat on the edge of her bed, the

light in the hall making enough light so she could see him clearly. He looked tired, but happy. His shirt was unbuttoned and hung over his dark dress pants. "Your mother and I talked about getting another foster child, and we've both agreed that we want to. We're still young, and we have a lot to offer."

"Yes, you do."

"Since we've had teens for so long, and still do, we decided we'd stick with that age group."

"I'm glad." Before she could say more Vera walked in, tying her dressing gown around her slender waist. "Mom, Dad was just telling me about your decision to get more foster kids. I think that's wonderful!"

Vera sat beside Chuck and reached for Elizabeth's hand. "I think it's wonderful of you to give up your room, but now that both Susan and Ben are gone, we'll have two rooms. So you keep this as long as you want."

"Won't you get tired of my hours of practicing while I'm here?"

"Never!" said Vera. "I could listen all day long."

"Maybe we should buy a baby grand piano so that you'd be able to practice on a good instrument," said Chuck.

Elizabeth laughed. "I'll help pay for it. Oh, how will I get to sleep now thinking about that?"

"I think when you close your eyes you'll be out," said Vera with a laugh. "We've all had a very busy time since you got home."

Later Elizabeth lay alone in her bedroom and smiled happily. Tomorrow she'd find the perfect baby grand and bring it home and play it. Then she'd be ready for her concert, for every concert that came along.

The end of July she walked on stage at Kramer Auditorium and the applause rang around her. She smiled and bowed to the audience, then sat at the piano, carefully arranging her dress around her on the bench.

A hush settled around her and she touched the ivory keys. She knew her family, her friends, and strangers who loved music were waiting to hear what she had to give.

She smiled as she struck the first chord. She was Elizabeth Gail Johnson, concert pianist! Her dream had come true.